KATHARINE ASHE

THE PIRATE & I

A Novella

AVONIMPULSE

An Imprint of HarperCollinsPublishers

Excerpt from *The Duke* copyright © 2017 by Katharine Brophy Dubois.

THE PIRATE & I. Copyright © 2017 by Katharine Brophy Dubois. All rights reserved. Printed in the United States of America. No part of this book may be used or reproduced in any manner whatsoever without written permission except in the case of brief quotations embodied in critical articles and reviews. For information, address HarperCollins Publishers, 195 Broadway, New York, NY 10007.

Digital Edition JULY 2017 ISBN: 978-0-06-264177-9
Print Edition ISBN: 978-0-06-264176-2

Cover art by Christine Ruhnke
Cover photograph © Jenn LeBlanc/The Killion Group, Inc.
Cover image © Shutterstock (chair detail)

Avon Impulse and the Avon Impulse logo are registered trademarks of HarperCollins Publishers in the United States of America.
Avon and HarperCollins are registered trademarks of Harper-Collins Publishers in the United States of America and other countries.

FIRST EDITION

17 18 19 20 21   HDC   10 9 8 7 6 5 4 3 2 1

To Sophie, Will, and Lydia—
with very special thanks.

Summer 1803
Bristol, England

"**P**romise, maggot!" his brother shouted into the wind.

Eyes clamped shut, Charlie shook his head. Water lapped at his hair dangling into the sea. His bare ankles and arms where they'd trussed him were in agony. Salt stung the wounds and clogged his nose.

He tightened his lips together.

"Promise!" Jo insisted. "Promise you'll tell Father it was your fault, or it's back under you go."

"*Never.*"

Charlie thrust the base of his tongue up against his throat just in time. A sudden plunge downward, his stomach rising as a wave slammed against him, shoving him sideways, and then there was nothing but horrible sound and panic.

Their jeers echoed through the water.

Dizziness swirled, black and heavy.

His lips burst open.

They pulled him up choking.

Hurling him onto his face on the deck, they laughed more as he retched and heaved and then curled up like a pill bug, offering his back to kick instead of his aching gut.

"Had enough, Charlie boy?" His ears were plugged with water; he didn't know which boy asked. Not his brother, though. Josiah's favorite name for him was maggot.

"Answer him, wart."

Another kick to the spine.

Charlie swallowed back his groan.

A hand grabbed his jaw, fingertips digging into his cheeks and yanking his chin up. His eyes opened to his brother's face an inch from his.

"You'll tell Father you broke the platen, little brother, or you're shark meat," he whispered.

"In—" he rasped and coughs wracked his body. His throat was raw with seawater, his stomach churning. "Your dreams."

Jo snarled. Thrusting Charlie's head away, he stood tall again. Four years older, he'd always been taller, bigger, stronger. *Meaner.* Jo set his fists on his hips and it made him look even bigger.

"He'll cave, boys," he said with a hearty grin. "But he's asked for one more swim. To help convince him."

A cheer went up from the idiot minions. Jo wasn't stupid. But his friends were imbeciles, no matter that all their parents also owned prosperous shops in London.

They grabbed his limbs and shoved him over the rail, headfirst as always. This time they didn't bother unfurling the line gradually. He dropped fast into the water—too fast to prepare.

No air.

His eyes opened to swirling hell. He struggled against his bonds. He shouldn't. He knew that he would use up his air faster. He'd read it somewhere. Somewhere . . .

His throat was contracting, panic surging.

A wave knocked him hard against the hull. He squeezed his lips together—tighter—tighter. He refused to drown. He'd never give Jo the satisfaction.

Never.

CHAPTER ONE

March 1823
Edinburgh, Scotland

Despite the rain and the infrequency of street lamps, as Esme Astell navigated puddles and shadows she was feeling remarkably well. Her first day at the meeting of the Society of Perfumers, for which she had spent half her life's savings to travel to from London, had not gone *catastrophically* badly, after all. Only *modestly* so.

Three shattered bottles of Eau d'Aurore was not such a high price to pay to become accidentally and abruptly introduced to her idol, Monsieur Pierre Poe, master perfumer and guest of honor at the meeting. Tomorrow morning after paying for the wasted bottles she would still have a full quarter of her life's savings left over to travel with him to Paris.

If he invited her.

Please, dear Lord, let him invite her.

Kindly Mr. George, her most avid customer at the shop

in London, had brought her this far. *"Your nose, Miss Astell, is the finest instrument I have encountered in years. You must not waste it in this wretched little shop on Gracechurch Street."* His letter to the president of the Society had insisted that, even though a woman—and a very young woman at that—she should be welcomed among the elite group of perfumers gathering in Edinburgh for this once-in-a-decade international event.

She must now take herself the remainder of the way to Paris. And she would, even if she could not afford the mail coach and had to walk the entire way. Except across the channel, she supposed.

If necessary, she would *swim*.

Rain seeped into the cracks in the toes of her boots, saturating her only pair of unblemished stockings as she hurried along, not closing her fine instrument against the scents that rose from the wet cobblestones. The alleyway's shadows were strewn with refuse that she did not wish to inhale, but unimportant streets in this part of town were bound to be dark and malodorous.

Anyway, bad smells did not bother Esme. She already had plenty of experience with foul-smelling refuse.

"Go have your little adventure in London, girl. Come harvest time, you'll be crawling back here."

Her uncle's prophecy had not come true, though. There had already been not one harvest, but five. Five years during which she had made sufficient income to share a tiny flat above a shop in Gracechurch Street and save a few pennies each month. Five years during which she had increased sales in the little perfume shop by four hundred percent. Yet her employer still would not increase her wages.

Now at this meeting she must not fail. If she failed, her younger sisters would forever be trapped on their uncle's farm.

Failure here simply was not an option.

And—Paris!

Everybody said Paris in the springtime was beautiful. Esme had almost memorized all the French phrases in the little book her friends had given her as a thoughtful gift to pass the time on the journey from London.

"Enchantée de faire votre connaissance," she said now to the rain, testing out her favorite phrase.

Enchanted. What a delightful way to express pleasure over making someone's acquaintance, as though it were a magical event. Every friendship should begin with a little enchantment.

She could practically smell Paris already.

Footsteps echoed behind her, splashing fast and hard through puddles, obviously without regard for soaking stockings. The alley was empty, the rain falling heavier now between the buildings that seemed to lean in upon each other from above. Edinburgh might be booming, but this dilapidated part in which she had been able to afford lodging obviously was not.

Deeper shadows loomed ahead. The footsteps were nearing.

Nearer.

Not slowing.

Esme threw herself toward the wall just as a man hurtled by. He ran fast—despite his considerable size—faster even than the urchins that nabbed fruit from the grocer's on Gracechurch Street. He wore no coat or hat, and his wet hair clung to his back below his shoulders that were broad and to which the wet shirt fabric also clung.

Not only his shirt clung.

With her back pressed to the stone, she watched the silvery darkness ahead swallow him.

She blinked as she stepped away from the wall. Never before in her life had she looked at a man's bum. She had not *intended* to. The tight, perfect ovals had flexed as he ran and her eyes had just gone there, like dogs to a bone.

It must be the effect of her enchantment over dreaming about Paris. She should *definitely* not be dwelling on those perfect ovals now, or risking her safety another minute in this deserted alleyway. She started off again.

More footsteps pounded behind her, this time many runners.

Jumping back to the wall, she watched them come. One carried a torch that illumined all five. She recognized them at once as members of the city's police force. In the finer neighborhood where the Society meeting was taking place, policemen could be seen everywhere. But these were the first she had seen here.

"Pardon, lass!" one shouted as they ran by.

"He's gone this way, lads!" another cried, and they streamed around the corner of the building, taking the glow of torchlight with them.

Esme moved into the center of the alley again, her step still light. Nothing could dim her giddiness tonight.

Paris.

Droplets of Eau d'Aurore had soaked into her when she had been trying to mop it off the floor and the Society president and Monsieur Poe. The scent arose from her damp skin now, curling musky rose and tangy citrus and a hint of cardamom into her nostrils. She felt like singing. And dancing. She would, just as soon as she removed her sodden shoes and stockings. A girl didn't need music to dance in the privacy of her own bedchamber, after all.

A man appeared in silhouette at the alley's mouth. *The criminal.* The shoulders were unmistakable.

Doubling back?

He paused, looked both ways, and then bolted straight toward her.

The policemen's shouts echoed nearby. Esme's sodden feet would not move.

Ten feet away the criminal dodged toward the opposite wall and slipped into a dark crevice in the stone. Forcing his wide shoulders back into the crack, he looked straight at her, lifted a forefinger to his lips, and shook his head once.

His long hair was tangled over his brow and thick whiskers. His chest heaved upon heavy breaths but otherwise he was entirely still. His glittering eyes were fixed on her face, warning.

She opened her mouth to scream.

The policemen crashed into the alleyway, only three this time and without the torchbearer, spraying rain every which way.

"Lass, have you seen a scoundrel run past?" one demanded, smacking his club into his opposite palm.

From the shadow, the scoundrel's gaze no longer warned.

It *pleaded*.

Three against one. And the three were armed with clubs.

"I haven't," she heard pop from her lips, then gasped.

Nobody heard her gasp; the policemen were already past her and disappearing around the alley's far end.

She was trembling. She had never lied in her life.

Poking his head out of the crevice, the man dragged his shoulders free of his concealment. In three strides he was across the street and upon her.

He was much larger close up, all dramatic long hair and thick shoulders and clingy shirt and powerful arms that came forward faster than she could draw breath. His hands wrapped around her head, big and very strong. And shockingly gentle.

"*Thank you.*" His voice was a criminal's, rough and low and intense. And English.

And familiar.

No.

It couldn't be.

Then, abruptly, his mouth was on hers.

For three seconds she was kissed—warm lips, firm intention, soft whiskers, and, amidst all the transient scents of rain and sweat and wet linen . . . *him*.

Esme's windpipe knotted itself around her heart.

Her ears occasionally lied to her. Even her eyes did. But her nose: *never*.

He released her.

Her damp lips fell open.

"Ch-Ch-Charlie?" she whispered.

Sparks flared in his eyes—beautiful, expressive eyes that she had thought she would never see again—eyes she had *missed*.

But there was no recognition in them. None whatsoever.

Frowning, he stepped back one pace. Then, without a word, he took off up the alley again at a sprint and was gone.

Her hands were shaking. Her entire body was shaking.

Charles Brittle.

Charlie.

He was alive.

Alive!

Since he had disappeared from London almost two years ago, no one on Gracechurch Street had seen him or heard from him. It had been entirely unlike him to simply go off without notice—or at all. Devoted to his family's print shop, hardworking, sober, and in truth the backbone of the business, he would never leave Brittle and Sons so suddenly, for any reason. So everybody on Gracechurch Street had believed him dead—fallen afoul of footpads, perhaps, but certainly gone forever.

Esme swallowed across her careening heartbeat.

Alive.

He had not recognized her. How could he have not recognized her?

Amnesia! It was the only possible explanation that he had never written to his family, and never come home to the shop where he was desperately needed, the shop that was his life. He must have been in a horrible accident and bumped his head and now had no idea who he really was, and so he had turned to a wretched life of crime.

But probably not.

Of course not.

Amnesia was a silly widgeon's justification for the months of grief she had silently endured when he disappeared. And she was definitely not a widgeon. She was on her way to becoming a world-renowned perfumer. In Paris.

Her friend Gabrielle had once told her that when multiple explanations for the same phenomenon existed, the simplest explanation was probably correct.

The simplest explanation now was that Charlie Brittle had actually always been as inconsiderate as his elder brother, Josiah Junior. Probably he had gone off on an unannounced holiday, discovered he preferred that to working day and night so that his brother and father could dress in expensive coats with gold watch fobs, and had forgotten about all of them back on Gracechurch Street who were waiting for his return. And missing him.

Now he was running around Edinburgh's dark streets and being chased by the police.

Now he was *a criminal*.

"Charlie," she whispered again, this time to the rain, and lifted her fingers to touch the lips he had kissed without knowing whose lips they were.

How many times had she dreamed of him kissing her? How many times had she stood in the window of her flat that overlooked Gracechurch Street, watching the door of Brittle and Sons, Printers, for his departure at the end of each day, and whispered his name when finally he came through the door, locked it behind him, and walked down the street to his family's house in a much finer neighborhood? How many times had she sighed his name, making fog against the windowpane and wishing that once he would look at her and see *her*, really *see* her, and realize that she adored him?

Too many. Far, far too many.

And when he had disappeared, her heart had broken—her foolish heart that had ached for a man who spoke to her every week for three years without ever really noticing her.

Now he was alive. *Not* an amnesiac. Simply inconsiderate. And a criminal.

Whatever his purpose in Scotland, and wherever he had been for two years, now meant nothing to Esme. Memories, regrets, and heartbreak were all entirely of her past.

Squaring her shoulders she walked the remainder of the way to the boardinghouse. After a good night's sleep she would stride into the meeting tomorrow and take all of those men by storm. She had her future to secure, and her sisters' futures too.

That future had one name: Paris.

The second day of the perfumers' meeting dawned sparklingly clear and blue. It passed much better than the first: she did not break any bottles of expensive fragrance, and

Monsieur Poe actually peered at her for at least ten seconds before he rolled his eyes away.

She did, however, make the acquaintance of several other perfumers she knew by reputation, and she soaked up lectures on saffron and sandalwood, on tropical blooms and wood resins, and on etched versus blown-glass bottles. She was so engrossed that throughout the day she almost did not think once of Charles Brittle's expressive eyes. And her mind was so taken up with modifiers, blenders, and fixatives that it had no opportunity to dwell on the surprising softness of his lips or the wonderful strength of his hands. By the time she was again walking along the alleyway in which she had abetted him in escaping the law, she was so filled with excitement about all she had learned that she did not even glance at the shadowy crevice in which he had hidden.

Gathering her bedchamber key and a smelly tallow candle from the boardinghouse proprietress, and promising she would wash up swiftly for dinner, she finally allowed herself to spare a thought for Charlie's welfare. If the police had caught up with him, he could be in jail. It would be a kindness to bring him a basket of food.

But she did not have time for that, or extra coins. All of her energies and thoughts now must go toward impressing the perfumers. And every coin possible must be saved for her journey to Paris. She had nothing to spare for a man who cared so little about his family and friends that he hadn't even informed them he was alive.

In her tiny bedchamber furnished with only a narrow

cot and her own small traveling trunk, she hung her cloak and bonnet on pegs and sat to untie her boots. Her room lacked a fireplace, and, like the window in her flat in London, the latch was broken so cool air seeped in through a crack and her shoes had not dried properly the night before. She slipped her damp feet free and reached for her indoor slippers.

With a creaking grind, the window sash rose and a man climbed through the opening.

Esme yelped, leaped up, and bolted for the door.

"*Halt.*"

That voice: low and harsh yet familiar. *His* voice.

Fingers clutching the door handle, she pivoted.

She had never thought Charlie Brittle a particularly large man. He needn't be: he was a gentleman. Five years ago, after arriving in London from the countryside—where every farmhand was ruddy and bulky—she had instantly admired Mr. Charles Brittle's pale skin and lean frame: markers of his gentility.

This man barely resembled that Charlie. He seemed to fill the room. In the golden glow of the candlelight, his skin was darkly tanned and his shoulders looked even wider than they had in the alley. Muscles strained his shirtsleeves, and his waistcoat barely contained a chest that was considerably broader than she recalled. He still wore no hat, but now his hair was bound in a queue, streaks of gold running through the sandy blond. His legs, encased in snug breeches, were set in a wide stance that revealed a wealth of taut muscle all the way down to his boots.

All muscle—the same as his backside.

Heartbeat punishing her ribs, she stared.

"Good evening, Esme." Lips framed in whiskers barely moved as the words came from them like a husky growl. His beautiful eyes were two hard, cool pieces of flint. "I need your nose."

CHAPTER TWO

That a piece of the past could be before him now seemed unreal to Charlie.

But there she stood, exactly the same; from her golden hair neatly plaited about her head, to her intelligent eyes and pretty lips, to the simple gown that hid her figure, she was the same Esme Astell he had seen every Wednesday when she came to the shop to collect her friend Gabrielle for lunch—the same Esme who had always greeted him with a glimmer in her eyes that suggested more beneath the blue-gray, and a "Good day, Mr. Brittle," yet barely ever another word.

Never before had he heard the hushed shock in her voice that had jolted him into looking clearly at her the night before.

Hours later, the brilliant idea had occurred to him.

Now she stared wide-eyed, candlelight making her eyes almost violet.

"I need your nose," he repeated. He had spent all day

tracking her to this boardinghouse, and another three hours waiting across the street to discover which room she stayed in.

"My *nose?*" Her voice was crisp and clear, nothing like the stuttering of the previous night. "Charles Westley Brittle, where have you *been* for two years? Everybody has been worried sick about you!"

The transformation from shock to indignant fury was so complete, he nearly laughed aloud.

But he never laughed anymore. Ever.

"Have they?" he said.

"Of course they have! Actually, truth be told, we all thought you were . . ." She blinked several times very swiftly. "Dead."

In fact he had nearly been dead, on any number of occasions.

"Listen," he said, "I haven't time to explain now. I—"

"Oh, haven't you? Then have you time to thank me for saving you from the police? Or to apologize for—for *accosting* me?"

"I beg your pardon," he said between clenched teeth. "That was a mistake." An impulse born of relief so thick he had acted before thinking.

Good God, for the first time in twenty-one months he had *acted* before thinking. That miserable pirate Pate would be proud. Pate had not christened him Scholar, after all, out of admiration.

"A mistake?" Her cheeks had turned a bit dusky. "What has *happened* to you, Charlie?"

"More than you can possibly imagine." The words sounded like an animal's snarl.

She had turned her face slightly askance and was looking at him as though he were little more than a dog. Of course she was. He was a dog. In fact, he had learned lately that he was worse than a dog.

"Now," he said. "Will you help me, or not?"

She faced him squarely again. She had a sweet little figure, with breasts that could fit entirely in a man's palms and a slim waist hidden by her dress.

But he knew the shape beneath that dress; he had glimpsed it once before, when she had volunteered to assist Gabrielle with a filing project in the office. Esme had crouched in front of a box on the floor, tightening the fabric around her soft buttocks and cinching it around her hips, and he had gotten hard in an instant. He'd had to sit at his desk for an hour to hide it until the women finished their work. But the following morning while shaving he had recalled the vision of her round behind, imagined that softness brushing against him, and his hand had gotten so busy he'd missed breakfast.

Callow dolt.

Now, as thought of the curves beneath her shapeless gown made his cock twitch to life, he met her gaze with a hard stare. A feral dog, after all, did not break a sweat over a pretty girl.

"All right," she said with only a trace of hesitation, but her fingers played restlessly in her skirt, as though they wanted to reach for the door handle again. She was nervous.

Good.

Keep a man off balance, Scholar, and you can knock him over easier.

Charlie had no intention of knocking Esme over. But he would not leave here without her promise to help him.

"All right?" he said.

"I admit that I am interested in hearing how and why you need my nose," she said, "by which I assume you do not mean my actual nose, rather my sense of smell."

He folded his arms.

Her sweet pink lips tightened.

"I will hear you out," she said. "But first you must answer one question."

He hiked up a brow. "Must I?"

"Yes, you must."

He'd had no idea her eyes could spark like that. *Intriguing.*

He tilted his head forward.

"Why do you—" Her nostrils flared as she drew in a visibly deep breath. "Why do you look like . . . that?"

"That?"

"All of—" She waved a hand roughly toward his midsection. "All of that hair and tanned skin and . . ." Her throat jiggled in a little swallow.

"And?"

"Muscles," she said quickly. Her gaze flitted away for an instant then returned even more direct. She folded her hands before her.

"I've been at sea," he said.

"At *sea?*"

"Yes. Interview over?"

"No."

"Pity, because I'm in some haste here, Esme—"

"I did not give you permission to call me Esme. Nor did I give you permission to enter my room. If Mrs. McDade discovers you here, in the morning I will be tossed out."

And if this woman did not help him, in a sennight he would be dead. Or worse.

He returned to the window and lifted a foot to the sill. "Meet me at the pub on the corner in ten minutes."

"No."

One boot on the ledge, he paused. "Why not?"

"I cannot go to a pub alone to meet a gentleman," she said as though he were daft.

"That's fine, then. Because once you meet me there you won't be alone." He swung his other leg out, balanced on the ledge, and ducked his head to peer at her beneath the frame. "And I'm not a gentleman." He winked. "Ten minutes, Miss Astell."

Dragging the window shut, he gripped the sill and dropped to a foothold below, then peered into the lamp-lit alley in each direction. Certain it was free of Edinburgh's finest, he swung down to the ground, hunched his shoulders, tucked his chin, and headed toward the pub.

At the door of the public house, a boy fell into step beside him.

"Got her, Scholar?" he said around the stick between his teeth, his freckled face turned up to Charlie.

"Yes, Rory. Now be about your business. And if you tell the others where she's lodged I'll have your guts for garters."

"Aw, Scholar." He kicked his toe into a cobble. "The lads wouldna tell Pate. They're all one hundred percenters for you!"

"It is for her safety *and* theirs, Rory."

The boy bared his teeth in a quick grin. "Aye, aye, sir." He scampered off.

Sir. As though he were still a gentleman.

He pushed open the door, scanned the taproom for potential danger, and, seeing nothing amiss, slid onto a chair in the corner.

She would meet him here. She had a much fierier temperament than he'd known. And an independent streak too; from what he had observed, she was on her own in Edinburgh. But she was still Esme Astell, Gracechurch Street shopgirl who with pretty smiles peddled cologne to men who thought they needed to smell like lilacs to get between a woman's thighs.

He knew that the lion's share of what she, Gabrielle, and their bosom bows, Mineola and Adela, gossiped about was men—his brother, typically, and the swells who patronized the shops on Gracechurch Street. When the four friends occasionally gathered for lunch in the pressroom, he had overheard them often enough.

Of the four, Esme was the most self-possessed. Her quiet reserve spoke of confidence and self-reliance. But the glimmer ever present in her eyes spoke of an irrepressible spirit.

The fewer words you say, lad, the less rope they have to hang you on.

Nobody from that pleasant world—his former life—would ever know the truth about what he had been through, the hell he had endured, the hell he himself had wrought.

A man could only go so far before the path behind him got washed away forever. He had long since crossed that point of no return.

This unexpected detour into the past was necessary, but it would be brief. He needed one thing from her, and when he got it he would leave again. This time, though, he had a plan: a new name, a new city, and a new profession. Once and for all Charles Brittle would disappear forever.

The following morning when he stepped out from behind a carthorse at the side of the road and took her arm firmly in his, Esme swallowed her gasp. The narrow footpath was crowded with people on their way to shops in the rain.

"What are you doing?" she rasped, tugging at her hand pinned between his hard biceps and equally granite ribs. She was not accustomed to being held in this manner by a man—or anyone. And this man was so . . . *hot*, despite the cold rainy morning.

She had never imagined Charles Brittle would be hot to the touch. And the most unnerving thing: she realized now that she had been covertly studying men's buttocks to compare them to his.

She fumbled her umbrella, and he snatched it from her fingers and held it firmly above her head.

"Why didn't you meet me?" he growled.

Today he wore a hat smashed down over his brow, and she could only see his nose and lips and whiskers. Even those looked displeased.

"I told you I wouldn't."

"Miss Astell," he said, navigating her around the corner as though he knew her destination. "Perhaps I did not make myself perfectly clear last night." His voice was like gravel. "I need your help. And I will have it, whether you wish to give it or not."

"That's high-handed of you, isn't it?" she said with more confidence than she felt. This man of extraordinary strength and rough vocals and threatening declarations was not the man for whom her dearest friend Gabrielle had worked for eight years. Obviously more had changed since he had left London than his hair and muscles. "I don't suppose it has occurred to you that I have a purpose here I cannot jeopardize," she said.

"I do not intend to jeopardize anything about you."

A little shiver of nerves scurried straight up her center.

"That is a relief," she said without any internal conviction whatsoever. She had spent hours the night before trying to fall asleep and instead imagining what might have happened had he not climbed back out of her window but had remained in her bedchamber—imaginings which had inevitably run to more *mistakes*.

"Name the place and time," he said. "If you do not meet me, I will come through the window again."

"The mews behind the old print shop at the base of the castle." Fantasy mistakes or no, she could not afford to lose the money she had already paid Mrs. McDade for the sennight's room and board. "Six o'clock."

He released her.

"Until then." With a bow that bent his big muscular frame more gracefully than she had thought a man of his present size could bend, and which was entirely at variance with his rough clothing and hair, he disappeared into the crowd.

The day at the perfumers' meeting passed as the previous day, in a whirlwind of lessons and scents that the masters had brought with them from their various homes. Of them all Esme preferred a delightfully subtle musk made from a base of Seville almonds and Provençal avocado oils, which a master from the Languedoc region of southern France presented. But when Monsieur Poe turned up his nose at it, she kept her opinion to herself. Later, when the Parisian perfumer asked her thoughts on another scent, and listened to her for a full minute before turning his attention to someone else, she felt so elated she wanted to dance.

At the end of the final lecture, though, she sought out Monsieur Cadence, the Languedocian perfumer, and complimented him on the perfume. A Frenchman, he had crinkle lines around his eyes and mouth, and the kind twinkle in his eyes reminded her of Mr. George in London, although several decades older; Monsieur Cadence was at least seventy.

"You are too kind, mademoiselle," Monsieur Cadence said. He had thin, oiled moustaches and a mother-of-pearl-rimmed lorgnette that reminded her of the great noble matrons who occasionally stopped into the Gracechurch Street shop. "It is a French name, Astell, *n'est-ce pas?*"

"It is. My grandfather was French. He married an Englishwoman, and then my father married an Irishwoman. So you see, monsieur, I am a mongrel."

He laughed.

"You remind me of my own granddaughter, who— *hélas*—I have not seen since she sailed to America. There is a delightful café on the corner. May I treat you to an aperitif?" He offered an arm clad in very fine gabardine. Monsieur Poe might not be impressed with his southern colleague, but Monsieur Cadence was clearly doing well for himself.

"If you promise to someday share with me the recipe for that divine scent," she said with a responding smile, "I would be more than happy to—*Oh.* No. I cannot. I'm afraid I have a previous engagement." With a criminal. "Tomorrow, perhaps?"

"Tomorrow it shall be, mademoiselle." He tipped his hat and she headed off to meet the man for whom her heart had broken two years earlier.

At present, however, that organ felt far from broken. Perhaps it was due to the knowledge that Charlie was alive. Or perhaps it was because she smelled like Sevillian almonds and had spoken directly with her idol *without* having first thrown a bottle of perfume on him. Or perhaps it was simply that she had spent three entire days soaking up not only scents but knowledge and ideas that she was eager to put into practice.

The rain had let up and the cobbles before the abandoned

stable sparkled beneath the setting sun. Charlie was standing in a shadow, his back against the wall, the hat pulled down over his brow.

Despite the muscles that showed through the taut shirt fabric of his crossed arms, he looked less intimidating than he had that morning and the night before. A trick of the light, she supposed.

But when she neared and he unfolded, she realized it was not the light, rather that it must be his intention to diminish the appearance of his size. She had seen him do the same after she ran to her window to watch him descend from it to the street like an acrobat. She had never before seen a man try to make himself appear smaller. He did it so effectively, like a magician's trick. She supposed he was, after all, still hiding from the police.

The Charles Brittle she had known in London had been the most respectably staid shop proprietor on Gracechurch Street. His elder brother, Josiah Junior, was entirely unlike him: a flirt and profligate of the worst order, with golden curls and a winning smile that teased customers and shop-girls alike. Charlie had been the rock, the honest, admirable heart of the print shop.

Now as he approached he removed his hat and his gaze fixed upon hers as it had in the dark and rainy alleyway. Another little spark of nerves raced up her torso.

Pleasure.

The tingly sensation flinging itself about in her stomach was, unmistakably, pleasure.

Adoring him in hopeless silence for three years had not

been pleasurable. It had been occasionally wistful and at times painful and always frustrating. But never pleasurable.

This was new. It was no doubt on account of the muscles. And the whiskers. A woman was bound to respond to all of that blatant masculinity with natural awareness.

Esme's passion and talent were entirely about the human senses. Also, she was half Irish and another quarter French. As such, unlike some of her English friends, she was not shy of physical sensation. Rather the opposite.

She *liked* this pleasure.

"So you decided to come," he said.

"Good evening to you too, sir," she said, tucking her hands into her pockets. "For what task do you need my nose?"

"Straight to the purpose," he murmured. "Good girl."

"I am not a girl. I am twenty-four." And on her way to becoming a world-renowned master perfumer. "What do you want of me, Charlie?"

He seemed to study her, a glimmer of something she did not recognize in the gold flecks of his beautiful hazel eyes. In the fading daylight she could see tiny white lines radiating out from the corners of his eyes, tracks in the tan.

"You never called me Charlie before."

"I didn't? I must have," she said.

"Not before two nights ago."

"Perhaps it is because before two nights ago you had never kissed me," she said with what she hoped sound like asperity.

"You didn't resist." It looked as though he smiled, but through the whiskers she couldn't quite tell. "Do you typically welcome kisses from strangers in alleyways, Miss Astell?"

"No. And you are singularly outrageous."

"When you lied to the police, you didn't yet know who I was."

"And when you left London you were deathly afraid of the sea."

His eyes shuttered.

"To the purpose, Miss Astell," he said in the low voice from that morning.

"I see. You are permitted to speak of the past and question me about kisses but I am not allowed to ask about your sudden disappearance and two-year silence or the astonishing information that you have been *at sea?*" It was impossible to stand so close to him and not be continually tempted to stare at his arms, which still lacked a coat despite the chilly night, and his sinew-corded neck, and even dip her gaze to his remarkable thighs. "I don't know what you have been doing for two years, Mr. Brittle, but it certainly has not had a particularly good effect on your manners."

"We can agree on that," he said.

Pinning her gaze to his face that somehow was much handsomer because of the tiny lines around his eyes, she saw now a slight bump on the bridge of his nose that had not been there before, as though his nose had been broken.

Someone had struck him. *Harmed* him. The idea hollowed out a little empty place in her belly.

"What do you need of my nose, sir?"

"I need it to find a dog."

Her eyes widened, the lashes fanning outward.

"A dog," she said. "An actual dog?"

He nodded.

"Any dog?"

"A specific dog."

"You wish me to sniff out a specific dog in the entire city of Edinburgh?"

"The dog's owner will be at a party in Leith tomorrow night."

"Leith. The port?"

"Two miles up the road. I'll provide transportation, and I will return you to the boardinghouse before your curfew." The tendons in Charlie's knee were strained against the impatient jitter that wanted to overtake his leg. But he had learned the hard way how to control that jitter; his back bore the scars that proved it.

Still, if she did not agree to this, he would have to devise a method of convincing her. That *kissing her* popped into his mind was proof of how little remained in him of Mr. Charles Brittle.

There was only Scholar now. And Scholar was short on time.

In the time before Pate returned to Leith, Charlie had a simple list of tasks to accomplish: find the dog, return it to its master, attend an auction at which a valuable collection of antique books was to go on the block, purchase the collection with every shilling he had managed to save over the past twenty-one months, then get the hell out of Scotland or anywhere else Pate could find him when he discovered the dog had been nabbed from its new owner.

The money or the dog, Scholar. Hand over either to me, and I'll give you the freedom you're so keen on.

Pate would discover that he'd stolen the dog—again. And he would come after him. But after he spent the money on the books, he'd have none left to pay Pate for his freedom.

He had to get that dog.

Any tactic that would secure the goal now would suit.

"Will you do it?" he said.

She blinked. "Mr. Brittle, unfortunately I cannot—"

He heard himself growl.

"Mr. Brittle," she said even more firmly. "Unfortunately, I cannot assist you in this task."

Men twice her size had cowered at his growl. But he hadn't time now to marvel at her fortitude.

"I have no money." None he could use for this. "I've nothing to buy your compliance."

"Buy my compliance? For goodness' sake, what are you—"

He stepped forward and grasped her elbows.

"If you do not assist in this, matters will proceed very poorly for me. Very poorly. I beg of you, Esme. Help me."

She tilted her face up and for a moment she simply stared at him. Then, with a flicker of her lashes, her attention dipped to his mouth. Longing shone in her eyes.

Longing? In *this* woman's eyes? No. Curiosity, perhaps. Uncertainty. Even skepticism. Not longing.

Yet if there were any emotion Charlie knew particularly well, it was longing. And Esme Astell's intelligent eyes were now full of it.

She wanted to be kissed.

He drew in a slow breath. If she wanted kissing to be convinced, he would do it. He had done much more for much smaller stakes before. And this time he suspected he would actually enjoy it. Her fragrant, unsmiling lips were a breath of freedom from a distant world.

Steeling himself for one last taste of sweet civilization to carry back into hell, he bent his head.

CHAPTER THREE

"I'll do it," she whispered with only two inches between their mouths.

He leaned back and released her arms, disappointment mingling with profound relief. Her lips were full and dark pink and he would have liked to have that memory.

"Thank you," he said.

"But I have two conditions." Again she folded her hands. She was unbelievably adorable, with her pert nose, the bonnet framing her golden braids, its ribbon tied at a jaunty angle beneath her chin, and her small, sweet breasts rising on the quick breaths she was trying to hide.

"What are they?" he said.

"Before I go to Leith with you, you must tell me everything."

"Agreed."

Both slender brows perked high. "You will tell me?"

"Yes." He wouldn't. Not everything. Everything would give her nightmares for months. But he would tell her enough to satisfy her curiosity. "If you agree to never share the information. With anyone."

"Anyone?"

He nodded once.

"I agree," she said.

"The other condition?"

"You must not enter my room through the window again," she said just a bit primly, her brows still arched high.

For the first time in months he found himself smiling.

"I agree to your terms, Miss Astell."

"I cannot remain here with you now," she said, glancing about the street. "I mustn't—that is, it would not be ideal if anyone saw me here with you."

A frisson of panic stole up his spine. Allowing her the night to ponder this agreement was not wise.

Always act quick, Scholar, and you'll never find a knife in your belly.

Pate's hated voice in his head had saved him a dozen times in twenty-one months. But it wouldn't guide him now. The crease in her brow made him back away. The tiny remnant of the gentleman inside him fighting to remain alive could not force her.

"By first light," he said, "leave word for me at the Hart and Rose as to where and when you care to meet tomorrow. I'll be there." Slapping his hat back onto his head and dragging it down to shade his eyes, he started off.

"Wait."

He turned to her. Her hands were clenched together at her waist.

"Tonight," she said.

"Tonight?"

"I will meet you tonight. At nine o'clock. At the Hart and Rose."

He hadn't smiled this much in two years.

"A woman of courage." He bowed. "Until nine o'clock, Miss Astell."

As he left the mews behind, his steps were easier than they had been in eons. Soon, very soon, he would be free—free for the first time in more than a year and a half. And she would make it happen.

She might not require a kiss now. But when this was all over, he would enjoy one all the same. In thanks, of course.

He was in fact no longer a gentleman. Far from it. And taking what he wanted was what a pirate did best.

After dinner Esme waited until Mrs. McDade was occupied receiving room keys from several women leaving the boardinghouse at once, and slipped past them. If the proprietress did not have her key, she would not know she was gone.

Inside the pub the rich, warm scent of stout mingled with coffee, black tea, bacon, and bread fresh from the oven. A bar in the center allowed the tables about the edges to each have virtual privacy.

"The corner table," she heard in her ear and swiveled her head to find Charlie not six inches behind her. A hot, wonderful wave of pure pleasure rushed through her.

In the past, seeing him unexpectedly had always made her heart do little skips and her breaths come too quickly. But these feelings he elicited—now—were entirely different.

He was just so *big*. And hard. She had never really noticed men's necks before, but now she could not seem *not* to notice that even this unremarkable part of him looked muscular, the sinews pronounced. Staring at it did deliciously wanton things to her insides.

The muscles of farm workers at home had never done such things to her. She supposed it simply must be Charlie's muscles, then.

He stood nearly as close as he had earlier at the mews when he had held her and she had thought he intended to kiss her.

He hadn't, of course. Charles Brittle would never in a thousand years kiss *her*—not intentionally, at least. He had, after all, said that kissing her in the alley was a mistake.

"Quickly now," he said in that same low, rough voice she could not quite believe was his. "We mustn't attract undue attention."

He looked like a laborer, yet still spoke like a gentleman.

She went to the corner table and began to slide onto the bench, but his hand came around her arm, stalling her.

"There," he said, nodding toward the opposite seat. "I've to keep a watch on the door."

Prickly alarm scampered around her stomach. *So many sensations.* It was like a banquet!

Shifting to the other side, she watched him fold himself into the bench with his back against the rear wall. His gaze scanned the room.

"Why must you watch the door?" she said. "Are you expecting someone else? Some other woman whose bedchamber you also broke into last night, perhaps?"

A gleam lit his eyes, but he did not smile. His smiles used to come infrequently, but they had been so warm. Kind.

This man *radiated* heat. But there was no warmth of sentiment in him now.

The barkeep set down a bottle, two glasses, and a pot of tea and a cup, then left.

Charlie poured from the bottle into both glasses. He slid one toward her. The piquant tang rising from it made her eyes water.

"Thank you, but I don't drink spirits," she said.

He took up his own glass and swallowed the contents as she poured tea.

"Will you ever ask me the reason I am in Edinburgh?" she said.

"It's irrelevant to me."

Setting down the teacup, she stood up. "Mr. Brittle, I came here tonight as a favor to—"

He grasped her wrist.

"I beg your pardon, Esme." His voice was very low. "It's been some time since I have had to—I beg your pardon."

In the golden flecks of his eyes was the oddest, most unsettling light.

She reseated herself. His hand slid away but remained palm down on the tabletop, as though keeping it at the ready to restrain her again if she sought to leave.

In two days now he had touched her, and said her name,

more times than he had in three years. He must desperately need that dog.

She took up her cup again. The steam rising to her nostrils soothed her.

"Did you know, of all the senses," she said, "smell is the most vivid enticement to memory? For instance, I can drink unadorned black tea every day and it will always remind me of sitting at the table in the old farmhouse with my sister Mary teaching our youngest sister, Colleen, how to hold a cup and lift it to her lips without spilling."

He simply watched her now, and did not respond.

"After many months of this," she continued, "when Colleen finally mastered it, my mother made cakes with the last of the sugar and we had a celebratory tea party." So many tears had been shed in those months, yet they were always intermingled with laughter and embraces.

Colleen had been four when she had begun talking. Five when she had first walked alone. Seven when she had first used a teacup and spoon without assistance.

In her last letter, Mary wrote that Colleen had just completed her first needlepoint sampler: three block letters on a scrap of old linen—*A*, *B*, and *C*—in time for her fifteenth birthday.

Esme's throat thickened. She *could not* fail in her project here. Whatever reason Charles Brittle had for hiding from the police, and no matter that his beautiful eyes made her insides dreadfully achy, she could not jeopardize the only chance she would ever get to save her sisters from their uncle.

"How I miss them." She sighed.

"Why have you come to Edinburgh?" he said below the conversations of other patrons.

"I am here for a gathering of perfumers," she said. "Every master perfumer in Europe is attending. I hope to apprentice myself to the best."

Charlie said nothing. She wrapped both hands around the teacup.

"I suppose you don't wish to hear about anybody else on Gracechurch Street either," she said.

"You suppose correctly." Oddly, his gaze seemed to be on her lips.

She licked them.

His fingers tightened about his empty glass.

"All right," she said, private little explosions happening where they probably shouldn't. "Tell me your story."

"It isn't a story. Merely a few inconvenient coincidences."

"Why did you leave London?"

"The shop was doing well. I hadn't had a real holiday in years."

Ever, in Esme's understanding. While Josiah gadded about town like a socialite and Mr. Brittle Senior negotiated deals with authors, Charlie did everything else: kept the shop stocked with supplies, organized the schedule of projects for the pressmen, designed layouts, set the type of every page, and ensured that each publication was flawless, each printing perfect. Esme's friend Gabrielle Flood, who had proof-edited pages in the shop for eight years, always said the business would fail if not for Charlie.

"Perhaps I should say, why did you leave London unexpectedly?"

But she knew. For all eight years that Gabrielle had worked at Brittle and Sons, Charlie had been devoted to her. Then one day a handsome naval captain had swept in and swept Gabrielle off her feet, and Gabrielle resigned from Brittle and Sons. Three days later, Charlie had disappeared.

"I needed a change," he said now.

"Did you find the change you were seeking?"

The line of his mouth amidst the whiskers was unforgiving.

She held her breath.

"I did," he only said.

She blew out a frustrated exhale. "Mr. Brittle, if you will not keep to your side of the bargain, I will not keep to mine."

"I rode to the coast, sold my horse, found the docks, and signed on with the first ship that needed hands. It happened to be a whaler." He spoke without inflection in his voice. "A month later our ship was boarded by pirates. I was—"

"*Pirates?*"

"I was impressed into the corsair's crew—"

"Im-impressed?" she stammered.

"Given the choice of life as a crewmember or death, I chose to live. I spent the next twenty months on board until I disembarked in Leith last week. End of story." Finally he moved, leaning forward until she could see each gold fleck in his eyes. "That fulfills my side of our agreement, Miss Astell. Recall that part of yours is to share the story with no one."

"You have been a *pirate?*"

"It's probably best not to inform everyone in this pub, hmm?" he said with a slight upturn of one side of his mouth. "We don't want anyone here to feel the need to summon the police. Then you might have to lie again, and I might have to kiss you again, and we would be right back where we were two nights ago, wouldn't we?"

"This cavalier attitude is not charming me."

"I don't need to charm you. I only need you to fulfill your side of our bargain."

A hundred questions tumbled to her tongue.

She made herself nod.

"Tomorrow night in Leith," he said, "the Assembly Rooms will host a public ball. The man currently in possession of the dog will attend that ball. I have not, however, managed to discover his name."

"He owns a dog you want, and you know he will attend a ball, but you do not know his name? That seems unlikely."

"And inconvenient. Yet it is the unfortunate truth. I also know nothing of his appearance."

"Charlie," she whispered, "you haven't really been a pirate for nearly two years, have you?"

"Focus, Esme."

"I am having difficulty digesting all of this."

"Clearly. But I have very little time to find this dog. Do you understand?"

"Yes. But how you expect me to find a particular man with a particular dog at a ball at which I assume there will be dozens of men, I cannot fathom."

"Men of wealth keep their dogs in the countryside. For hunting."

"I see. But if you don't know who the man is, how do you know that he is wealthy?"

"He paid another man a significant sum to steal the dog for him."

"Oh!" Relief fanned through her. "He did not come by the dog honestly?"

"No. He has been in possession of it only a few days. Are you satisfied now that I am not dragging you into performing quite as reprehensible an act as you imagined?"

"If I had imagined you were dragging me into performing a reprehensible act I would not have come here tonight, of course."

He seemed to study her, his features hard. But now in the gray-green of his eyes she saw an intensity of emotion that shocked her.

"Why don't you run away?" she blurted out. "You are on land now. You can leave for London in the morning. Go home. Your father and brother will help you. The shop is as successful as ever. It's true that they were at wits' end for a few months after you departed, and Gabrielle left, of course, and they had to scramble around a bit to replace both of you. But they did so, not as competently as either you or Elle, but sufficiently. Your family must have plenty of money to—"

His gaze shifted over her shoulder. She swiveled to see five boys entering the pub.

"You lads," the barkeep said. "Be off with—"

"They are with me," Charlie said in the deep voice that made Esme's insides shiver with heat.

The barkeep grumbled and returned to wiping the bar.

Four of the boys remained just inside the doorway. One came forward, his eyes widening.

"Knock me down, Scholar! She be a bonnie one!"

"Stuff those eyes back in your head," Charlie said. "Miss Astell, this is Rory Markum of the Blue Thistle in Leith."

Rory's spine went straight. "How d'you do, mum?" He tugged on the brim of his filthy cap. Then he spoiled the effect by offering her a grin that lacked all four front teeth. He was wiry and no more than nine or ten.

In the doorway, the other four boys tugged their caps too.

"Good evening, boys," she said.

"Did you boys come here only to gape at a pretty woman or do you have information for me?" Charlie's features had settled into sober lines.

"Aye, sir. Pate's fixing to come ashore as planned."

"Five days."

"Aye." Rory screwed up his lips. "Got a plan, Scholar?"

"I do. Now off with you. And keep your ears to the wind."

"Aye, sir!" With another tug of his cap at her, and a wink, he scampered out with the other boys.

"Your minions?" she said.

"Just boys in need of activity."

"Mm. That was what you used to say about Sprout."

"Did I?"

"Gabrielle told us that when Sprout was about to be taken

by the sweep master you hired him to run errands for the shop. She said you saved Sprout."

"She overstated it."

"I don't think so. Who is Pate?"

"Nobody important."

"And if he were you wouldn't tell me anyway, I presume."

"You presume correctly."

"Why did Rory call you Scholar?"

"Sailors are fond of nicknames," he said and leaned forward again. "I never realized you were so curious."

"That does not surprise me," she said with a little curve of her dark pink lips. "You barely ever spoke to me. Not directly."

Because after that occasion with the filing project and her round hips and his fantasies, every time he looked at her he'd forgotten what he intended to say.

"Curiosity, now," he made himself say, "will not serve you well, Esme."

Her lips were parting and her lashes fanning and, *blast*, his breeches were tightening.

"I have realized why it is that you believe I can find the man with the dog," she said.

"Have you?" His voice was too rough. For all her tightly braided hair and simple gowns, she must know that when men looked at her their mouths went dry.

And when she smiled . . .

The whole room got momentarily hazy. Those lips . . .

Focus, *Scholar*.

"Yes!" she exclaimed. "When Sprout lost his puppy, *you* began the hunt for it. You must remember how I found it in the Barrel."

The King's Barrel was a three-story rabbit warren of rooms and nooks and corridors. Yet Esme, a girl accustomed to the scents of bergamot and roses, had sniffed out the mongrel hiding in an old crate.

"Yes," he said.

"It was nearly midnight before we found it," she said with a delighted grin. "But you would not give up searching."

Neither would she, long after her friends had gone home.

"You knew how Sprout adored that pup," she said. "How kind you were to him." Her eyes looked too bright. "Charles Westley Brittle, you are a good man."

He grasped her hand, gripped it tightly, and made his tone neutral.

"If I saw that man on the street today, I would not recognize him. You asked me why I do not leave for London?"

Eyes wide, she nodded.

"I cannot go home," he said. "For any reason. Ever again. The man who left London twenty-one months ago is dead. Believe that." His hand slid away from hers. Setting coins on the table, he stood and waited for her to follow. "I will walk with you to the boardinghouse."

"Yes," she said, taking up her bonnet, covering her golden braids with it, and moving toward the door. "You must. I cannot enter without your assistance."

When he stepped out onto the street he said, "I beg your pardon?"

"For a man who claims to be a pirate, you still speak remarkably like a gentleman. I suppose that is why they call you the Scholar?"

"Just Scholar," he corrected and bit back his smile.

"Mrs. McDade bolts the front door at ten o'clock. The clock in the pub showed quarter past ten just now."

"That would have been useful information to have twenty minutes ago. Where exactly do you expect to sleep tonight?" He shoved away images of her golden tresses spread across his skin.

"In my room. You must teach me to climb in through the window."

He grasped her elbow lightly, and she halted and turned to him. Pale light from the lamp at the Hart and Rose's door illuminated her eyes and damnably fine lips, which were smiling now.

"You planned this," he said.

"Of course I did. If we are to be free to take whatever time necessary tomorrow night to retrieve the dog—do you know its name?"

"No."

"We will call it Argos."

"Argos?"

"From ancient mythology," she said as though of course he knew that. Which he did.

He released her. "Odysseus's dog?"

"Suitable for a pirate."

"Odysseus was a hero, Esme."

"He was a sailor. Anyway, if we are to be free to take

whatever time necessary to retrieve Argos tomorrow night, we mustn't be worrying about my curfew. A rehearsal tonight is wise."

"How do you propose to climb up the side of the building wearing that?"

She looked down. "Do you think my skirts will impede movement?"

"I think there is a reason sailors don't wear them."

"Oh, is that the reason, Mr. Scholar?"

"Just Scholar." He didn't want to wait for the excuse of the police chasing him: he needed those sassy lips beneath his now. And then the rest of her beneath him too.

Abruptly her brow pleated.

"Is it very uncomfortable?" Her voice was unsteady.

Tamping down lust? *Yes.*

"Is what very uncomfortable?"

"Sailing away from land, when you fear the sea?"

Extraordinary. For three years he had believed her sweet, reserved, self-possessed. And edible. All that time she had been hiding *this*.

"Not any longer," he said.

"How did you do it?"

He headed toward the boardinghouse.

"Enough questions for tonight, Miss Astell. You've a building to scale."

Chapter Four

She cinched her skirts up between her legs and he did not even blink. He taught her how to find finger holds and how to set her toes at the best spots, all the while glancing up and down the dark alleyway. Every sound she made seemed to echo between the walls. But her bedchamber was only on the second floor.

"How did you come to be such a proficient climber?" he whispered behind her.

Countless flights into the hayloft dragging her sisters behind her, escaping their uncle's rod, and he always too ale-sodden to follow.

"I grew up on a farm," she threw over her shoulder, digging her fingertips firmly into the ledge of her windowsill. Stepping up to the final nook, her foot caught in her petticoat.

Abruptly, his hand was encompassing her buttock.

"Steady now," he said quietly.

How he expected her to remain steady with her behind in

his big, strong clasp, she'd no idea. She gripped the sill with one hand and tucked her fingers beneath the sash, which earlier she had left partially open, and forced it wide. Then his hand on her behind was propelling her upward and through.

She tumbled over the sill and onto the floor. As she untangled her skirts, he appeared in the opening.

"I did it! Albeit with help." Her cheeks were in flames.

"You did it. And fell on your face, yet you are laughing." It was too dark to make out his features, but he sounded as though he were smiling.

"I feel positively triumphant." And her behind could still feel the sensation of his hand around it, which they would quite obviously never speak of. "It's nearly as cold in here as out there." She climbed to her feet and he passed her cloak to her. "I must shut that window. Are you coming inside?"

"You forbade me from doing so."

"So I did." A wise precaution. Minutes ago on the street below she had considered grabbing him and kissing him. As an experiment. To see what it would be like to kiss him unaccompanied by the shock of simultaneously discovering he was alive.

"Seven o'clock tomorrow at the Hart and Rose," he said.

"I will be there. You should cut your hair and whiskers. And buy a coat. The police would not recognize you so easily."

"You are taking to this life of crime with remarkable ease."

"In for a penny."

"I daresay." He reached up to the sash and the moonlight behind illumined muscles straining the thin linen sleeve. A delicious fluttering took up a dance in her abdomen.

"You asked how I did it." His voice had changed. It was no longer smiling.

"Yes."

"Do you remember the day the performing troupe passed along Gracechurch Street, and everyone went outside to watch?"

She remembered every detail of that day. It was the last time she had seen him, the day before the worst weeks of her life, when every hour it seemed more certain that he had perished.

"Yes."

"The first time I set sail," he said, "as I watched the land disappear, I remembered your words from that day."

"*My* words?"

"Sprout had never before seen a fire-eater. He was astonished. He asked how the fellow had the courage to do it."

"I remember."

"You replied that courage is no more than surviving fear from one moment to the next. Then you told him how three years earlier, without any knowledge or experience of the world beyond the farm, you had set off to London, and of how terrified you were. You said that as you walked you gave yourself markers on the horizon ahead, and that each time you reached each marker, yet had not yet swooned of fright, you accounted it a triumph."

"I did not know you were listening," she whispered.

"I thought of those words that first time I sailed, and every time I left land behind after that."

"Did you give yourself markers on the horizon?"

"At sea there are no markers that remain still. I used clouds and pretended they did not move. At night I used the stars." He lifted his other arm to grasp the sash. "Good night, Esme."

He pulled it shut.

When she had fastened the faulty latch, drew the curtain closed, and removed her boots, she changed into her night-gown, curled up beneath the thin blanket and her cloak for warmth, and closed her eyes. It had been an astonishing day. Yet, unremarkably, sleep was some time in coming.

The light carriage that Charlie drove up to the Hart and Rose was not the finest equipage Esme had ever seen. But it was not the shabbiest either. And the horse looked capable.

"I did not know you knew how to drive," she said as he extended his hand to assist her onto the box. She took it and the shock of pleasure in feeling his strength went straight through her.

"I have all sorts of unexpected talents." The glint in his eyes was thoroughly suggestive. Gone was the pensive man from the night before. The light of early evening cast his features into a perfect semblance of handsome roguery.

"You shaved off the whiskers! And cut your hair. And it is black!"

He snapped the reins and the horse started off. "You required a change in appearance."

"And you bought a coat."

"Stole a coat."

"You *stole* it?"

"Pirate."

"Yes, but you needn't—that is—Do you intend to return it? Someday?"

He offered a quick sideways smile. "I do now."

"Did you steal the horse and carriage as well?"

"Borrowed."

A mound of earth connecting old Edinburgh to newer suburbs had been constructed across the marshy loch that had once divided them. At dusk as in daylight it was a beautiful city. Esme had already posted a letter to her sisters and mother describing it and the Society meeting, and of course Charlie's miraculous appearance.

She stole another glance at him.

"Why are you still smiling?" she said.

"I wish you had spoken more often in London."

"I don't know what you mean. I spoke plenty in London."

"Not to me."

"Perhaps I did, yet you simply did not notice it."

"I would have noticed."

As he had noticed—memorized—her words to Sprout that day. Nerves raced around her belly.

He had been in love with Gabrielle. For eight years. That day the troupe came by, Adela mentioned how Gabrielle would have been happy to see it, and he had said he suspected Gabrielle was sufficiently happy already with her naval captain. He had seemed so somber, and Esme's heart had hurt for him.

Then she had gotten angry, at herself for holding out the

tiniest hope that now that Gabrielle was gone he would see *her*. Finally.

The next day he had disappeared and she had forgotten about her anger and instead mourned.

"What is our plan tonight?" she said.

"Young Rory is to meet us. He'll have arranged what you need to gain entrance into the party."

"Am I to wear a ball gown and pretend to be a lady?"

"Would you enjoy that?"

"Oh, yes. I adore dancing."

"Do you?" The smile returned.

"Dancing at fairs and such." They were sitting very close. If she shifted her thigh even the slightest bit, it would touch his. "I have never before attended an actual ball." She could reach out her hand and stroke that muscular thigh . . .

"Tell me about Argos," she forced through her lips and turned her gaze forward.

He glanced at her briefly. "Argos?"

"You must know something of the dog itself since you know nothing of the man who now possesses it. How else will you be certain which dog to steal?"

The muscles in his jaw contracted. Esme was obliged to concentrate so intently on restraining herself from extending her hand and stroking her fingertips over those muscles that she started when he spoke again.

"It is small. And white."

"How do you know that?"

"The fewer questions, Miss Astell, the better."

She pinned her lips together and faced forward for the remainder of the journey.

Shortly, standing in the alley behind the enormous Assembly Rooms building, Rory did not produce a ball gown. Instead he proffered a black dress, cap, and apron.

"A maidservant?" Charlie said with a frown.

"I tried to nab a lady's turnout, sir," the boy said with an earnest pleat in his grubby brow. "Got the stockings and dress. Come to find out, a lady wears a whole mess o' fripperies 'neath her skirts! Who knew?"

"Who knew, indeed?" Esme smiled.

"When ol' Pickle offered me this instead," Rory continued, "I supposed it'd be easier to slip into them here in the alley anyway. Right, miss?"

"Much easier." She accepted the garments and glanced about. Except for some empty crates by the assembly hall's rear door, the alley was bare from end to end. "But where, here, precisely?"

Charlie moved behind her. "Here." His hands came around her neck and he was unfastening the clasp of her cloak before she knew what he was about. He withdrew it from her shoulders. "Boys," he said, "make a circle and turn your backs. And if any one of you peeks, I'll string you up by your thumbs to that lamppost. Understood?"

A chorus of "Aye, sir!" responded.

Charlie lifted the cloak between them.

Esme had never before undressed and dressed again so swiftly. When she finished, she pushed the cloak aside.

"How do I look?"

"Like a proper serving maid!" Rory chirped. The other boys nodded.

"Lads," Charlie said. "Take the gig and find a safe location to wait. We'll see you back here in two hours."

The boys leaped into the carriage and drove it away.

"They are far too sweet to string up by their thumbs," she said.

"You haven't seen what else they are capable of." He was obviously restraining a smile. "Are you ready?"

"Perfectly."

"I am sorry you will be obliged to actually work."

"Aha, so you think. But you haven't seen what *I'm* capable of." As she pulled open the door, she winked.

They entered a kitchen, a large chamber filled with people dressed in livery like hers, all pouring champagne and ladling out punch and washing glasses. It was a beehive of activity.

The moment she closed the door, an elderly man in black livery said, "You there! The main chamber at once." He took up a tray laden with full champagne glasses and thrust it at her.

She accepted it and he turned to another.

First hurdle crossed.

Balancing the tray carefully, she went from the kitchen and through a little antechamber.

And into paradise.

High-ceilinged and painted a glorious buttery yellow, the ballroom was lined with mirrors that made the whole place sparkle with candlelight from crystal chandeliers. A festival of scents spun in her nostrils—beeswax, floral perfumes, musky colognes, sweet wine, and bodies—so many scents Esme felt dizzy. And every soul present was more beautiful than the next. Women glided by in gowns of light, shimmery fabrics, their hair dressed with tiny flowers and silk ribbons and even jewels, and gems twinkled on their necks and ears and around their gloved wrists as well. The gentlemen were equally resplendent: many wore black from shoulder to calf, which according to Minnie was popular evening dress lately, and their neck cloths gleamed white, some even decorated with jewels or gold pins.

And the dancing! Esme had only ever dreamed such a vision: the lightness of the ladies' feet, their skirts swirling and swishing, and the elegance of the gentlemen's move-ments, the masculine hand on a lower back here to support his partner, or there grasping delicately gloved fingers . . .

Magnificent.

It was like a fairy tale.

"Try not to spill, Cinderella," she heard at her shoulder, then Charlie moved past her and into the crowd. He carried a tray of beverages as well and wore footman's livery, including a short coat that perfectly revealed his tight bum.

Steadying the tray upon which the champagne was now washing back and forth in time to her swaying, she set off into the crowd.

Cinderella.

Cinderella actually got to dance, and she had not been looking for a man who smelled like a dog among dozens of men. But she had made a bargain. And watching the dancers was a treat. She could not wait to write to Mary and Colleen all about it.

Circulating through the room, Charlie kept his eye on her. It was not difficult. Among the beautiful women present, she was the only one wearing servants' garb. No wise employer would actually hire a maid with such speaking blue eyes and an enticing figure that moved fluidly, gracefully, as though she needn't even a partner to dance. Enough male eyes followed her progress through the crowd that Charlie knew other men were thinking the same.

Men being what they were, he suspected it would not be long before some scoundrel too far into his cups insulted her.

From across the room he watched her head swivel, then to the other side, then her sweet body turn slowly. Then her gaze came to him.

Charlie had been punched in the gut on many occasions, and in the face, and on one shoulder shortly after being shot in that shoulder, and in the knees as well. Seamen weren't much for teaching lessons with verbal chastisements.

Meeting her gaze now he felt punched, beneath his ribs, deep in his organs, the breath shooting out of him and pain radiating. Everything was muffled—the music, conversations, laughter—as though in a dream.

Then he was again at the edge of the ballroom, staring at her and trying to understand why his heart was beating so swiftly and so hard.

"You there" came a voice beside him. "Give me one of those, do."

Shaking his head to clear it, he turned and offered a glass of champagne to the woman.

"By golly," said the man beside her, looking past Charlie. "If it's no' the Duke o' Loch Irvine come out o' his lair."

The noise in the ballroom had fallen to a hush, only the musicians still piping and fiddling as everyone's attention turned in one direction. Even the dancers craned their necks.

From the base of the stairs, a man was making his way along the length of the ballroom. Tall, dark, and dressed in equally dark evening attire, he had the shoulders of a stevedore and he walked across the ballroom like a captain walked across his deck: like he owned the place and everyone in it.

Around Charlie, people were whispering.

"—returned—"

"—the nerve o' the villain!"

"—in plain sight—"

"—never imagined—"

"It seems the rumors are true," the woman behind Charlie whispered to her companion. "The Devil's Duke has returned to society."

"Big fellow, ain't he?" the man said. "Believe the rumors o' abducted maidens and whatnot, do you?"

"Of course! He is notorious, never mind that he is a duke."

At this moment the notorious duke was walking straight toward Esme.

Everybody had begun to talk again, still throwing glances

at the duke as he paused at the door before the beautiful serving maid who was, in fact, a talented perfumer.

The hairs on the back of Charlie's neck bristled.

Shoving his tray of glasses at a passing footman, he made his way through the crowd, his attention pinned to the pair.

The duke took a glass of champagne from Esme's tray, drank it in one gulp, and spoke directly to her. She laughed, her eyes like violets in the candlelight and her rosy lips curving. Red washed across Charlie's sight.

In another moment he was beside her and the shadowy duke was gone into the foyer beyond.

"There you are," she said. Her eyes were full of sparkles. Charlie wanted to make them light up like that. He wanted to make her laugh. He wanted to put that pink flush on her cheeks.

"I see you've spoken with the Devil's Duke," he heard himself say roughly—*too roughly*.

What in the hell was happening to him?

"The who?"

"That man who just left. The Duke of Loch Irvine. You spoke to him."

"He was a duke?"

"A notorious duke, apparently."

"How wonderful! I have never spoken to a duke before. Once I sold a bottle of Violets of the Glen to a marchioness. And Lord Witherspoon regularly comes into the shop, but I don't think he is an actual peer, rather the son of a real lord or something. Adela and Minnie know a lot more about lords and such than I do. Was that man really a duke? And notorious? He seemed a bit bemused, perhaps, but otherwise entirely normal."

"Normal?" He smiled. "Esme Astell, you are a remarkable woman."

"If by *remarkable* you mean remarkably talented, it is true. For I have already discovered no fewer than seven men who most certainly have spent time with a dog since last they bathed."

"Have you?"

"Of course I have. Charlie, have you been drinking that champagne instead of giving it to the guests? You look peculiar. And you are behaving oddly."

He was. And standing so close to her with the heat of irrational jealousy in his blood was not helping matters.

"Seven?" he managed to say.

"Yes. There," she said, looking pointedly at a tall man nearby. "That man with the military medals on his coat. And that man with the lavender pantaloons. Lavender: can you fathom it? That florid one with the red waistcoat. And that man with the shirt points up to his nose is another. And the man with the plaid across his shoulder. And the man speaking to that young lady wearing that unfortunate gown with five rows of lace. Minneola would split something internal if she saw that gown, I think."

"That was six."

"And the duke that just walked by. But he is well under forty. I like systematical studies, so I began with the eldest gentlemen in the room and had only just gotten through those who seemed above the age of forty. Oh, and the duke's dog must be very clean. I barely smelled it, and only because he was standing so close."

Charlie's collar felt twelve sizes too tight. And not two yards away a young fellow in a fashionable rig was eyeing her as though he'd something on his mind other than a glass of champagne.

He took the tray from her hands and set it aside.

"It is time to leave."

Her brows perked high. "But I haven't sniffed any man below the age of forty or so."

"You needn't." He would let her get close to the young men over his dead body. "This is a good start."

"But what if he is not one of the men I identified? Aren't you short of time?"

"It will be fine." It wouldn't. But that hardly mattered. He should not have embroiled her in this. "Can you give the boys now the details as you have just described the seven men to me?"

"Of course. But what will they do, prowl about the carriages asking questions?"

"Something like that. Now, best to leave before anyone finds us out." And before he did something irrational, like invent further uses for her nose so that when he returned her to the boardinghouse he would not have to say goodbye to her forever.

CHAPTER FIVE

Esme's companion was quiet on the return drive to Edinburgh. His clean-shaven jaw looked remarkably hard, and his hands were tight about the reins. They had left their servants' garb with the boys and he wore again the stolen coat and distractingly tight breeches.

She was riding through the dark with a criminal.

This she could not tell her sisters in any letter ever.

"What will you do next?" she finally said.

"Retrieve the dog."

"Steal the dog," she corrected. "How will you track down seven men in all of Leith and perhaps even Edinburgh?"

"Rory and the boys will. They are clever. And they know this port."

"They are impressively loyal to you."

"They're good boys."

"They are thieves," she said lightly. "And that was not an answer."

"Eight months ago," he said, "when we briefly made port at Leith I found two of Pickle's colleagues mistreating Rory."

"Mistreating?"

Muscles flexed in his jaw.

"This Mr. Pickle is a low fellow?" she said.

"The lowest. But he has his uses."

"Thus our servants' garb tonight. What did you do when you found them mistreating Rory?" she said.

"I made it clear that they'd not want to be bothering young Master Markum again." After a moment he added, "It was not a new experience for me, Esme: beating men until they were begging for mercy."

She knew he said it to shock her.

"It wasn't?" she said a bit thinly.

"No. Where I've been these two years, I swiftly learned that it's eat or be eaten."

Yet he had intervened to rescue a stray boy from harm. She stared at his hands in the light from a lamp on a passing building—powerful hands that had once set tiny pieces of metal carefully into a printing press tray, hundreds of pieces in perfect order, to create books of extraordinary beauty.

"How swiftly one can have experiences one never before imagined possible," she said. "I feel thoroughly steeped in new experiences tonight. I have seen a real ball and I have served champagne to lords and ladies and I have worn stolen clothing."

He glanced at her. "I am sorry to have brought you into this."

"Don't be! I had a wonderful time."

"You wanted to dance."

"I did." She drew a deep breath and looked up at the sky glittering with stars. "When Mama was particularly unwell, Mary and I used to pretend we were great ladies attending a ball. We would tie old linens around our waists as ball gowns, and make chains of flowers for diamond necklaces, and dance for her in the barnyard. It was to make Mama laugh, but sometimes Colleen would dance with us, and that made all of us laugh even harder. Colleen is a very poor dancer, which of course is understandable given that she can hardly even walk. So you see, I fulfilled a lifelong dream tonight to see a real ball. It does not matter that I did not actually dance."

"How did you do it?" he said.

"Dance in the yard? We never did after a rain, of course. The mud would have ruined our shoes. But on dry days it was easy. Mama had taught me the steps."

He smiled again. "How did you identify the seven men with dogs?"

"Oh." Of course he was not interested in the silly games she had played with her sisters. "It was not difficult. Warm-blooded animals are incredibly smelly."

"Are they?"

"Oh, yes. Every animal has a particular unique scent. But each creature also has incidental scents that are either superficially layered onto the unique scent temporarily, such as the scent of a dog on a man's coat or hands, or imbued, such as the scent of spirits in a man's skin."

"You can smell all of that?"

"Especially incidental scents. For instance, in London you—"

"*I?*"

"You smelled of printer's ink, which is acrid, and wool, which is rich and textured, and occasionally metal, iron specifically, but only after you set type, I believe. Now your incidental scents are salt and—well—whiskey. But the whiskey scent is not imbued, rather superficial, thank goodness."

"Thank goodness?"

She drew in a deep breath. "My uncle drinks spirits. Quite a lot."

"I see." He glanced at her. "And what of my unique scent?"

"Oh, well, that is the same as it always was, of course." Like no other man's in the world. And it still made her dizzy.

"What is it?"

Little tingles erupted all over her body.

"I cannot describe individuals' unique scents." *Not* true. "I can only recognize them."

"That is how you knew it was I. When I kissed you."

"Yes."

It seemed that he might speak but his lips closed again.

"I am peculiar," she said. "I know you must think that. Most everybody does, except other perfumers."

The carriage came to a halt in the alley behind the boarding-house. He hitched the reins to the peg and leaped down.

"I do not think you are peculiar," he said, then came around to her as she descended. "Ready to climb?" he said with a smile that turned her stomach inside out.

She climbed, and this time her foot did not slip and he did not have reason to grab her behind.

"Let me come in," he said from the other side of the window.

"Why?"

"For that dance you are longing to have."

"Dance? Here? In my room? Charles Westley Brittle, don't be silly."

He threw a leg over the ledge, then the other. Sitting on the sill, he paused.

"May I?"

"Yes." She could not seem to stop staring at his thighs. His posture served to define the muscles with breathtaking clarity. "But tread softly. I have discovered that the floors and ceilings are thin."

He came toward her. "Has the resident above been dancing at night?"

"No." *She* had. And the resident below had complained of it to Mrs. McDade.

Then he was standing before her, so big and tall. By the pale late-winter moon's light his tanned face seemed both infinitely alien, like a stranger's, and dearly familiar.

"May I have this dance, Miss Astell?" he said and his voice seemed rougher even than usual these days. "Is that how your sister used to ask?"

Whorls of pleasure cavorted about in her stomach.

She nodded.

"Then what do you respond?" he said.

"I must consult my chaperone. Oh, how convenient: she

says I may. Yes, thank you, sir. I shall be delighted to dance with you."

"And now what?" A smile played about his fine lips.

"I curtsy and you bow."

She curtsied.

He bowed.

Then without prompting he offered his hand, and quite easily she summoned the courage to place hers on his palm. In her dreams she had, after all, done so many times.

His fingers closed around hers and she felt the most unusual sensation: the sensation of being *touched*. Since leaving her family she had rarely touched anyone; she had not been held or cherished. She had told herself not to miss intimate touch, trained herself to enjoy the sights and sounds and most especially the scents of her new life.

Now this man's hand around hers was a revelation. She had *missed* being touched. Heat and a magical sort of breathlessness filled her. Absurdly, she thought she might weep. Charles Brittle was holding her hand, truly holding it, yet at *this moment* she would cry?

She pushed back the sob gathering in her throat and met his gaze.

"What dance shall it be, madam?"

"I only know the reel and Speed the Plough."

"Then Speed the Plough it is."

"Why that one?"

"A dance that allows a gentleman to hold a lady more frequently is always preferable."

"Is it?" Her stomach was a flight of swallows.

"Of course."

"You have experience with this, then?"

"Vast experience."

She had never imagined Charlie attending balls, or any sort of party. She had thought him far too dedicated to work.

"Are you teasing me now?"

"Perhaps." His eyes were smiling. "Shall we?"

"We have no music."

"Do you sing?"

"Poorly," she admitted. "But I know you do."

"How, may I ask, do you know that, Miss Astell?" he said, leading her into the pattern, although much more slowly than an actual dance.

"From Christmastime, the first year I was in London." She had been desperately missing her sisters and mother. Gabrielle and Charlie had taken her to the King's Barrel for lunch on Christmas Eve. When Adela and Minnie joined them, they had all sung carols to lift her spirits. And they had. "But I suppose carols hardly serve at a ball."

"Then sailor songs it must be," he said, and began singing. "'Come over the hills, my bonnie Irish lass. Come over the hills, to your darling. You choose the road, love, and I'll make the vow, and I'll be your true love forever.'"

There was no roughness to his voice now. Smooth, deep, and beautiful, it softly filled the little room.

"'Red is the rose that in yonder garden grows—'"

"Sailors singing about gardens?" she interrupted. "That seems unlikely."

"'Fair is the lily of the valley,'" he continued with a grin.

"'Clear is the water that flows from Boyne. But my love is fairer than any.'"

"I was under the impression that sailors sing love songs to their ships."

"Always about women, usually women they've lost to other men while at sea."

"How sad!"

"''Twas down by Killarney's green woods that we strayed,'" he continued singing, "'when the moon and the stars they were shining. The moon shone its rays'"—he slowed the words, drawing them out—"'on her locks of golden hair.'" The pattern brought them face-to-face. "'And she swore she'd be my love'"—he paused—"'forever.'"

They had come to a halt close together and he was looking into her eyes.

"But he does not lose the woman in that song," she said.

His gaze, lit by moonlight slipping through the window, was traveling over her features. "He does in the next verse."

"Did you learn it from an Irish sailor?"

"Paddy O'Malley. He had a wretched voice. He told me he was the only man in his family who couldn't sing to earn a ha'penny. The others aboard wouldn't allow him to sing, but he missed the old songs."

"So you learned them," she said. "To sing for him."

"Did I?" he said with a quiet smile.

"You might be a pirate, Charles Westley Brittle, but you are one of the most decent men I have ever known."

"If you knew what I was thinking now, you would not think me so decent."

"What are you thinking now?"

"That I should like to see your locks of golden hair unbound."

The breath shot out of her. "You *would?*"

He nodded. In the shadows of the dark room she could see his throat move in a rocky swallow.

"I could unbind it now," she said.

Chest rising on a thick breath he said, "That would not be a good idea."

She took the step that brought her only inches from him.

"You are a pirate, Scholar," she said, tilting her face up. "You are not supposed to be good."

Slowly, he lifted his hand and curved his palm around her cheek. Bending his head close to hers, he paused, and she heard him breathe a long, slow pull of air, and it was all sweet, expectant wonder and perfect—*perfect*.

It was nothing like the first time in the alley. This time she was not cold and wet and alarmed. This time she was hot beneath her skin, expectant. His touch was so gentle but there was fever in his eyes.

"Go ahead and do it," she whispered so close to his lips. "I shan't break."

When he smiled there were lines of pleasure about his mouth that the whiskers had hidden.

"As you wish," he murmured.

He brought their mouths together. His lips were soft and met hers gently once, then twice, then a third time. It was lovely. Sweet. It sent tingles of pleasure all along her shoulders. He kissed her again, this time on the corner of her lips, then on the rise of her cheekbone, then so softly on her temple.

He drew back.

For years she had dreamed of really kissing this man. This fleeting taste was not enough. Now she wanted more. Much more.

She curled her fingers into his coat sleeves, pushed up onto her toes, and pressed her lips firmly against his.

With a groan, he sank his hand into her hair and took her mouth whole.

Neither of them hesitated—not for even a moment. Lips parting, she tasted his heat and song and desire in this mingling of flesh that felt like heaven. With the power in his hands he held her to him.

Wrapping her hands around his arms, she met each kiss eagerly, tasting him as he tasted her, and her senses were full of his flavor and shape and delicious male texture. Where her skin was soft, his was scratchy with whiskers. It made a wild agitation bloom inside her. He sought her closer, deeper, and she was melting—melting in hot, wet, wanton *need*. With a touch of his lips, with each kiss, he was feeding it. She had *never* imagined this, not from him, not for her. But she had wanted it. Longed for it. For years she had ached for him, wanting and waiting and yearning. Now he was filling her with pure, decadent lust.

Her nipples were prickly and needy, as though they wanted to be pressed against something. Against *him*. He was kissing her lips, one, then the other, playing with the inner seam of them with his tongue. She opened her lips to play too, and he entered her.

A moan of pleasure slipped over her tongue that he caught with his lips. Then he stroked her tongue again, and again. Between her thighs she was hot and pulsing. This was what she had wanted, needed, forever. This touching that was more than touching. This caressing inside, his body so close she could lean forward an inch and be touching him all over while his tongue was inside her mouth. She wanted to be consumed and to consume him.

Why couldn't she?

Her hands came between them, sweeping across then delving beneath his coat. Hard contoured muscle met her palms and delicious echoes cascaded into her thighs. She spread her hands and dragged her fingertips down his chest.

He broke them apart and his hands fell away from her.

"I'm leaving," he said roughly.

"You—"

"Now." He backed to the window. "I am leaving now. Thank you for your help tonight, and for the dance, and the—" He caught his breath. "Goodbye, Esme."

Then he was gone, out the window and down to the street and into the carriage so swiftly that by the time she poked her head outside he was already driving away.

Chapter Six

The little cottage had no bell or knocker, so for the second time in a fortnight Charlie rapped on the door panel.

The first time he had come here, of course, he had crawled through a window.

A crumbling abode of two uncertain stories, with rose vines and ivy vying to overtake the stone, nevertheless it boasted a neatly swept stoop and cheerful curtains peeking out from windows that were kept clean. He already knew that, inside, the furniture had once been fine but was now ancient and in need of repair, the walls showed darker squares where paintings had hung but had since been sold to pay for necessities, and the kitchen cupboards were nearly bare. This was genteel poverty, of the sort from which his father had come and about which he had warned his sons throughout their lives.

Not for the first time Charlie imagined Josiah Brittle Senior's horror were he to discover how far his younger son had fallen.

The door remained closed. He tested the handle, found the door unlocked, and entered.

In the cozy front parlor the woman, wrinkled and white-haired and far too light of flesh, was sitting in the same rocking chair in which she had greeted him the first time he had called on her, swathed in soft blankets that swallowed her.

He crouched down beside the chair.

"Mrs. Wallis," he said quietly.

Her eyes opened. Like many elderly folks' eyes, they were moist, and hers were pale blue. They crinkled as her face lit with pleasure.

"Dear boy," she said. "How delightful of you to call." She made movements to stand and he went to her side and assisted. The Englishwoman was all skin and bones, thinner even than a sennight ago, and much paler too. "Have you come for more biscuits? That lovely Mrs. Allen sent another batch yesterday, and heaven knows I cannot eat them all myself."

"I would not think of eating them without you."

"I will brew some tea."

"I will brew the tea," he said, and guided her to a chair in the kitchen onto which she sank with a grateful sigh. He reached for the kettle and lit the stove from the single oil lamp burning in the entire house. "You should lock your door, Mrs. Wallis."

"What is the use of living in the country if one must lock everything up tight as a sinner's bible? And now that Douglass is gone," she added upon a weak sigh, "I've no cause to care who comes or goes."

Remarkable how guilt could feel like an awl drilling a hole in a man's ribs.

"He will return. I am certain of it." He set the teapot on the table before her, and two cups.

In general he did not care for tea. On his previous visit he had come on the pretense that he was looking for work—carpentry, painting, repairs to be done about the house. She had promptly invited him in for tea, a lonely old soul seeking company wherever she could. On that occasion he had learned that she would not drink or eat unless he did too.

"As I entered," he said, "I noticed the exterior wall of one side of the house needs a fresh coat of paint. May I?"

"You have already done enough, dear boy."

"Yet more needs doing." The house was in sore need of refurbishment, but the widow had no funds to hire help.

"Haven't you a sweet old grandmother who needs your help more than a poor old stranger?"

"I've no one." Which was true. "And you are no longer a stranger."

After purchasing the books at auction, he would have a dozen or so guineas to spare. He would hire Rory and the boys to see to this house's restoration. They needed honest work, and it would keep them away from the docks.

He poured the tea.

"Now if you will, ma'am, tell me again the story of your spoiled nephew who ate through an entire fruitcake in one evening."

"Did you enjoy that story?" she said with a smile.

"I enjoyed how the little brute was ill for days afterward."
Her nephew had reminded him of Josiah, all selfish, brassy
bravado.

Mrs. Wallis's eyes twinkled. "You've a rascally soul,
Charles."

"That I do." He knew that now, at least. Taking her hand,
he curled it around her teacup. "Now, ma'am, on with your
story."

The following morning after too few hours of sleep, Esme
greeted the master perfumers with tired eyes but exception-
ally good humor. After taking a cup of coffee with Monsieur
Cadence and engaging in a spirited debate with several other
members of the Society, she listened to two fascinating
lectures during which her mind continually tried to wander
to the kiss, but she did not allow it.

Her purpose in Scotland was not to become a silly widgeon over a man she would never see again simply because
they had shared an earth-shattering kiss. It was to impress
Monsieur Poe.

With that in mind, she spent the remainder of the
morning attending to every word he spoke and trying not to
cringe when he insulted other perfumers and turned up his
nose—literally—at yet another of her favorite fragrances.

At lunchtime the president of the Society called a recess
for the afternoon to allow for a meeting of the directors, and
Monsieur Cadence invited her to luncheon with two other

perfumers. Afterward, as she walked home to the boarding-house, she finally allowed herself to think about the man who had kept her mind whirling till the wee hours.

He was gone, off to find the dog and then perhaps to sea again. She would never know where he went, nor whether he had escaped the danger that had inspired him to seek her help. Instead she would forever remember that kiss and the fever in his eyes when he had bid her goodbye.

Charles Brittle had kissed her. It had unsettled him.

She had not expected either—ever—not of the respectable London printer nor of the fugitive pirate. She was fully prepared to tuck it away as a confusing and breathtaking memory when the pirate in question came walking toward her.

Relief filled her alongside a very unwise euphoria.

"What are you doing here?" she said. She was still many blocks from the Hart and Rose.

"Good day to you too, Miss Astell." He was gorgeous, all tan and big and now smiling at her with only his eyes. Yet he moved the same as he always had, without ostentation. His brother, Josiah, always burst into a room, like sunshine when one suddenly pulls open the draperies. Not Charles Brittle: he never demanded attention, never raised his voice above conversational level, never shouted or ranted or lost his temper.

She had fallen in love with him because of that. Because he had been as different from her uncle as two men could be. That she realized this only now as he fell into step beside her created an odd, disconcerting ache in her chest.

"I thought I would never see you again," she said.

"Yet here I am."

"Why are you on this street?"

"I was on my way to investigate this Society of Perfumers. Why are you walking away from it?"

"You wish to investigate the Society?" she said in disbelief. "Why?"

"To ensure your safety. Who are these men, after all, who invite a young, beautiful woman into their midst, without a matron in sight? It is disgraceful. Scandalous. I intend to get to the bottom of it."

"Charles Westley Brittle, you are—"

"Overprotective. I know. I have heard that before. From Gabrielle. Also blockheaded and dull, although those insults came from my brother, who is an idiot, so I always discounted them."

"I was about to say wonderfully amusing." She lifted a brow. "But if you prefer criticism . . ."

He smiled.

Butterflies did country dances beneath her ribs.

"You are not concerned about my safety at the Society."

He shook his head.

"Why not? For I am, in fact, the only woman attending."

"I have no doubt, Miss Astell, that you are capable of making wise choices."

"Wise choices? Such as dressing up in stolen clothing and pretending to be an employee of a public hall and climbing up the side of a building?" And kissing a pirate beyond all modesty.

"Precisely," he said.

Pleasure skittering all across her skin, she started walking again. "The meeting is in recess this afternoon."

"How did you receive an invitation to it?"

"Questions now? I thought my business was irrelevant to you."

"I require your assistance."

The words made her far too happy. "Again?"

"I've need of a decent set of clothing."

"And you wish me to help Rory and the boys steal them? From one of the *perfumers?* Charles Westley Brittle, I will not jeo—"

"Jeopardize your purpose here." He was smiling again. "How is it that you know my middle name?"

"I—I don't know. I must have heard someone say it. Mrs. Brittle perhaps?"

"Speaking of my mother, although I am somewhat ashamed to admit it, she used to purchase my clothing. She enjoyed doing so, while I did not. I would appreciate your assistance in a trip to the tailor."

"And before demanding that I help you—again—you thought to make pleasant conversation about the Society."

"That's about the size of it."

She pinched her lips over her smile. "Be off with you, ruffian, before I summon a constable."

They paused at a corner for a cart to drive by.

"In truth," he said, glancing down at her. He wore no coat today, and his jaw was lightly shadowed with whiskers, the hat pulled down over his dye-darkened hair and shadowing his eyes. "How did you arrange to attend the meeting?"

"That nice man who often shops on Gracechurch Street, Mr. George, wrote a letter of introduction for me to the president of the Society."

"You traveled to Scotland alone on the faith of a man you barely know?"

"I have spoken to him more than I have ever spoken to you, in point of fact," she said, and crossed the street. "Gabrielle told us that you do not trust other men easily."

"Given my brother's habits with women, I have good reason."

Neither needed to mention aloud now how, years earlier, Jo Junior had cruelly used and hurt Gabrielle.

"Do you intend to return to London?" she could not resist asking. When he had first disappeared, she did not blame him for leaving the moment Gabrielle went off with her naval commander. But she had thought, *hoped*, he would eventually return. "Ever?"

"No."

Her stomach abruptly tied itself in knots. "You sound certain."

"I am. I have had enough of my brother and that shop for a lifetime."

"I understand."

"You do?" he said with a glance at her. "You are fond of your siblings, are you not?"

"Oh, yes. I am here for them. Rather, for me and for them. And my mother."

"I don't understand."

"Their situation at the farm is—well, it's not ideal. I had hoped to earn enough to support them in London until my sister Mary could find work too, and together we can care for Colleen and our mother. But Mr. Skinner refuses to increase my wages. So I have come here to find a successful perfumer who will take me on as an apprentice. It is the next step to becoming a master perfumer."

"I see." He seemed thoughtful.

"But when I said you have no reason to return to London, I was not referring to your brother, of course. She is no longer at the shop. Why would you return?"

"She?"

"Gabrielle." She walked three strides during which he did not respond and then she said, "You were in love with her, of course."

He glanced at her. "I? With Gabrielle?"

"Yes."

"I cared for Gabrielle," he said. "She is a fine person. And she was a good friend. But I'd no stronger feelings for her, Esme. Rather, I was in love with besting my brother at something."

She halted before the boardinghouse and he did so as well, and her heart was beating very swiftly.

"But you . . . We all thought . . . We believed you had strong feelings for Gabrielle."

"You all?"

"Minnie was convinced of it."

"Minneola Dawson has a vivid imagination and a flare for drama." He was looking into her eyes. "Deny it."

She laughed. "I cannot." A marvelous lightness was filling her up, lifting her feet off the ground until she was on her toes. "You never cared for Gabrielle as more than—that is, as more than a dear friend?"

"Perhaps I considered it. Occasionally. And I will not deny that my decision to set off to sea was influenced by her departure with a famous naval hero. But nights on the watch, Esme, hours and hours in silence and darkness lit only by a million stars . . . Nights like that allow a man plenty of time to think."

"I imagine they do."

"During those endless hours, Gabrielle Flood was not the woman who commanded my thoughts."

Abruptly there was no city street, no hawker on the corner selling tickets to a museum exhibition, no flower girl selling winter violets or other pedestrians or the noises of horses and carriages. There was only Esme's wildly beating heart and an enigmatic message in his usually expressive eyes.

"Scholar! We've been looking all over for you!" Rory came to a sliding halt beside them, three of the other boys in his wake. "Where've you been, sir?" he panted.

"Strolling with a lady, as you can see. Greet the lady, now, boys."

All four of them tore their hats from their matted hair and made excellent attempts at bows. Rory's bright blue eyes were trained earnestly on her face.

"Good day, miss! We returned the clothes well an' good as you wished last night, none the worse for wear."

"Thank you," she said.

He blushed to the roots of his grubby hair, then turned again to Charlie.

"We found out five o' the six, sir, no' counting the duke. Ronnie be hunting down the last."

"Good work, boys."

"Why not the duke?" Esme asked.

"The Devil's Duke be too far gone in wickedness to grab a wee dug, miss," Rory said with a wise nod of his head, then returned his attention to Charlie. "The one with the purple trousers, John Foxcombe, lives in a flat with his mum just up the street here. The boys n' I'll—"

"No. I will take it from here."

"Aw, now, Scholar. You'll have all the fun while the lads an' me dinna get none?"

"I'll not have you nabbed for stealing, Rory, not even for stealing back what has been stolen. Now tell me the names of the five and directions for them."

They did so. After instructing the boys to meet him in the morning at the Hart and Rose, Charlie sent them after their comrade Ronnie in search of the seventh man's identity.

"Why do the boys really call you Scholar?" she said. "And don't brush off the question this time."

"On board, whenever I finished my work, I read." The pleasure had gone from his voice and eyes. "And when we took other vessels, I searched for books."

Her stomach felt sick. "I suppose pirates do not typically loot other ships for books?"

"Food, livestock, and fresh water. Firearms. Ammunition. Gunpowder. Navigational charts. And gold, of course."

"I am coming with you."

His eyes arrested. "Coming with—"

"To Mr. Foxcombe's flat."

"No."

"What do you intend to do if his mother is home? Burst in looking all—all . . ."

"All?"

"Big and coatless and—and *pirate-like*, and simply demand she hand over the dog?"

"I'll manage."

"Don't be absurd. This is not the open sea. This is a thickly populated city. She might scream—why, *he* might scream, and twenty people would come running in an instant. Then your neck would be in a noose and I would weep bitterly into a kerchief as I watched you hang and then of course I would be obliged to break my promise not to tell anyone on Gracechurch Street about what happened to you, and I would never forgive myself for that."

"For that? You would never forgive yourself?"

"Of course not. I am an honest woman from the countryside, where the worst sorts of crimes we must face are an occasional chicken theft. You, a scurvy brigand, could never understand that."

"I am not scurvy."

"Why do you need—" Glancing at his waistcoat she was

immediately reminded of the hard muscle beneath it that her hands had explored the night before. Her cheeks heated. "That is—why must you go clothes shopping today?"

"If all goes well with this dog situation," he said in an entirely altered tone, "within the sennight I intend to board a ship to Boston."

The air left her lungs.

"Boston?" She hardly knew how the word came forth without air to propel it.

"There is a position waiting there for me. A modest position, in truth, but mine if I arrive by summer."

"What sort of position?" she said, not entirely steadily.

"In a rare book shop. The position is merely clerk, to keep the ledgers and such. But I will be glad for it."

An exceedingly uncomfortable mélange of confusion and despair was clogging her throat.

"But why would you go all the way to Boston when your family owns a hugely lucrative business in London?"

"I already told you, Esme. That life is over for me. I will never return there."

A carriage clattered by, and by the time it had passed she was able to say with credible élan, "Shall we make our way to Mr. Foxcombe's flat now?"

"I will. You will not."

"Charles Westley Brittle, I am not the wilting violet you seem to imagine I am, whose will crumbles beneath a man's glower."

"I imagine nothing of the sort."

"Come along then," she said, moving away from him. "No reason to delay."

"If we are caught you will lose your welcome with the Society."

"Then we mustn't get caught. *Obviously.* What sort of pirate are you anyway? For heaven's sake, it seems I have more natural criminal instincts than you, after all."

He only smiled, and Esme told herself to be content with that, and with a few more hours of his company. Before she boarded the mail coach for London, and he a ship for America, she would steal as many hours with him as she could.

Just like a pirate.

Chapter Seven

He should not have allowed her to come, especially as her prediction that Mr. Foxcombe's mother might be at home came to nothing. She did, however, distract the footman at the door to the building sufficient for Charlie to slip by and up the stairs.

Leaving her below with the fellow was enough to make his molars grind. She had never fluttered her lashes at *him* like that. But the moment the footman glanced away, her pointed look at him and jerk of her chin toward the stairs gave him no other option.

She was tenacious. And adorable. And the less he looked at her anyway the less likely he was to pull her into his arms and take up that kiss where he'd left off.

He had just entered the flat when a soft footfall sounded behind him and he pivoted.

"It is I!" she whispered, her eyes entirely round as she stared at the dagger in his grip.

He resheathed the weapon and turned again.

"Never sneak up behind me."

"I shan't," she whispered fervently. "It seems my criminal instincts aren't quite as good as I had thought."

The flat was empty except for two dogs enclosed by a fence in the kitchen.

Esme leaned close to his shoulder.

"Is either Argos?" she said into his ear beneath the cacophony of snarls and howls.

He turned his head. Her eyes were pools of perfect periwinkle, her lips a man's fantasy, soft and shapely. The night before he had discovered those lips to be far from passive recipients of kisses.

He needed to taste them again. Now. Every surface of his skin was hot, every muscle in his body primed, every thought insisting he must.

Instinct shouted *no*.

They had to get out of this place before the neighbors noticed the barking.

But, by God, the pink flowers rising on her cheeks and the quick lifting and falling of her breasts were shoving aside the instinct that had helped him survive at sea for twenty-one months; they were telling him to drag her into one of those bedchambers they'd passed on the way to the kitchen and do with her what needed to be done without delay.

She leaned closer. Her lips were inches away. Her eyes were unfocused. He could practically feel her body against his already, and her wet, hot mouth on him.

"We must go," she whispered.

Then she was gone, hurrying back to the flat's door and out and down the stairs. He followed more slowly, locking the door, then readjusting himself as he descended. He paused on the flight above and, over the railing, watched her sidle up to the footman and speak softly to him.

Then her hand was on the man's lapel, he was grinning and putting *his* hand on her arm and she was allowing it, moving closer to him, turning him to face the other direction. Charlie understood what she was doing, but prickly heat swept up the back of his neck and fanned across his shoulders.

Leaping down the remaining steps, he slipped past the pair and out of the building and was halfway down the block before he stumbled to a halt.

His breaths came quickly—too quickly—memories clamoring forward of every time Jo had stolen from him, so easily, always without effort, from extraordinary seashells found on the beach to his first fine quill pen to his favorite chair at the King's Barrel to their father's trust. Every time his brother had made a grievous error in the shop—ruined a page, broken a machine, lost an account—he had blamed it on Charlie. And because Charlie had never stood up for himself, their father believed Jo.

When just after Jo departed on a business journey Gabrielle came to work at the shop, Charlie had struck up a fine friendship with her. Then Josiah had returned and she had instantly fallen head over ears for the golden boy of Brittle and Sons. At the time Charlie had been hurt, but unsurprised.

It had required several years and the intervention of a naval captain for him to realize that somewhere along the way he had come to see Gabrielle as yet another *thing* Josiah had taken from him—not a woman with a heart and mind of her own. The realization had sickened him to the core. So he had ridden to the coast and signed on with the first ship he saw, determined to reclaim at least one treasure that his brother had taken from him: the sea.

Watching Esme walk toward him now with a quick step and bright eyes, he knew the reason Josiah had never tried to have this beautiful woman. Esme Astell had never interested Jo because Jo had never known that his little brother wanted her. Because his little brother had been too much of a coward to do anything about it.

"That was exciting!" The pale spring sun shone on her skin and in her smile. "Shall we search another dog man's house now?"

"No." His voice was recognizably husky.

Her gaze dipped to his lips.

"Last night," she said, "we kissed."

She was perfect.

"I noticed that," he said.

"I just thought I would put that out there."

"In the event that I had forgotten?"

"In the event that you want to do it again. Back in that flat it seemed perhaps that you wanted to. Again. For I surely do. Do you?"

"Yes."

Her lovely eyes flared.

"We won't," he said.

"Not here and now on the street, of course." She had dimples. He had never noticed her dimples before. They were shallow and only appeared when she was trying not to smile with her teeth.

"Not anywhere," he corrected. "Ever."

"Why not? Are you disgusted by my plain speaking?"

Rather, he was hard as rock, standing on a footpath on an Edinburgh street in broad daylight.

"Wanted criminal," he forced through his lips. "Leaving in days. What part about those don't you understand?"

"Well, you needn't be insulting. All right. That is fine then. I have no intention of throwing myself at you, Charles Brittle. So you need not worry on that score."

"I hadn't planned on worrying. But if you prefer that I quiver in—"

"Ha ha. See how I dissolve in laughter? Now, what sort of clothing do you wish to purchase? The sort of unremarkable garments you were fond of—that is, that *your mother* was fond of in London? Or another sort?"

The sort that would make a perfumer with a quick tongue turn to hot honey in his hands again.

"The sort a Boston shop clerk with pretentions toward better would wear," he said.

She simply looked at him, without pleasure or displeasure on her features, rather thoughtfully and with the reserve that in another reality he had thought was her natural state.

"On my first day here," she finally said, "I walked past a shop that will probably do."

She took him to New Town. Constructed on elegant, mammoth dimensions, with neat footpaths and a view of the castle cresting the older part of the city, the neighborhood boasted finely dressed pedestrians and pricey carriages. Before a particularly grand façade she came to a halt.

"That is a hotel," she said. "Inside it is magnificent, all gilded rose and ivory. Someday when I return to Edinburgh as an actual member of the Society, I will take a room there and dine on pheasant and champagne every night."

There was such determination in her face, and hope.

"You deserve it," he said.

"Not yet. But someday I shall. Now to the little tailor shop to remake you into a respectable gentleman." Her gaze dipped to his legs. "Respectable . . . Yes." Pivoting away, she set off up the street.

It was indeed a little shop, not much larger than the front room of Brittle and Sons. She selected a coat and waistcoat that suited Charlie's purpose ideally. He stood on the dais while the tailor poked pins into his wrists, and she watched from the other side of the shop. A dart marred the bridge of her nose.

Abruptly she turned away and opened the shop door.

"Where are you going?" he said. "There are still trousers to be chosen."

She looked over her shoulder.

"If you imagine I will watch you fitted for trousers, Charles Westley Brittle, you were not listening carefully to me earlier." She looked at the tailor. "Thank you, sir." Her gaze returned to him. "Mr. Brittle, I will see you at the pub tomorrow—if, that is, you do not disappear again without warning."

With perfect poise, she shut the shop door behind her.

The tailor paused in his work.

"Do you care to go after her, lad?"

"No."

But he did care. And that was the trouble.

In the mirror he stared at himself in the first gentleman's garments he had worn in nearly two years, clothing that would ensure his entrée into the auction two days hence. Before then he would find the dog. And after it, he would do exactly as Esme had suggested: leave town before Pate came looking for him.

Hot kisses were not reality. His debt to Pate was. There was no way in Hades he would put her in further danger.

"I seen him with the dug, miss!" Rory's eyes were bright, his sunken cheeks red from running. "No' an hour since, right here in town."

"You saw one of the seven men with the dog in Edinburgh?" Esme said. "The actual dog?"

"Aye. Ronnie and Davie be watchin' the house so we dinna lose him." His eyes scanned the pub's patrons. "I couldna find Scholar at the Thistle."

"I have not seen him today." Although she had stopped into the pub for tea in the morning and had returned as soon as Mrs. McDade removed her dinner plate from the table.

Her frankness about the kiss must have disgusted him. He was avoiding her. Or he had left town.

Or he was in trouble—injured or in jail or in some dreadful situation because he was a criminal and running from the police and beholden to whatever awful person wanted the dog. She could not bear the thought of it.

"We must go to the house and retrieve the dog ourselves, Rory."

"Aye, miss."

"No."

Charlie stood in the doorway wearing the clothing he had purchased the previous day. He looked like the man she had fallen in love with five years earlier, yet bigger, rougher, his shoulders broader and his eyes flinty again.

"Of course I will go," she said.

"No. You have done enough."

"Without me, you would not have come this far. And, Charles Westley Brittle, if you were hurt and I could have prevented it I would never forgive myself. You don't want that on your conscience, do you?"

"Charles?" Rory exclaimed. "Named after kings, you be, Scholar!"

Charlie was looking at her peculiarly. "I don't have a conscience any longer."

"Be that as it may," she replied, pulling her cloak over her shoulders. "I—"

Then he was before her and brushing aside her hands and fastening the cloak clasp.

"I cannot deny a lady," he said quietly.

Yet he already had, refusing to kiss her again.

She hoped he had regretted it all night.

As though he knew her thoughts, he smiled, slowly. "Shall we be off?"

Rory told them the street, and Esme knew it at once as a fashionable residence in New Town. Darkness had fallen and they hailed a hackney, and Rory marveled at the fine upholstery and speed of the horses. It was not a particularly fine cab, but he had never ridden in one before. Charlie folded his arms over his chest and watched the boy with quiet pleasure.

The carriage finally halted on a crescent of beautiful houses. A finely dressed gentleman walked up the steps and was admitted immediately. Through the doorway Esme glimpsed a man in neat livery, and an elegant foyer. She reached for the door handle.

Charlie stayed her hand.

"Wait." His hand over hers was large and she had the urge to twist her wrist and meet him palm to palm. Her breaths shortened.

"Why?"

"Study the situation before walking into it."

Acutely aware that he was not releasing her hand, she peered out. The knocker was brass and pots of spring flowers decorated the stoop. Draperies were drawn across every window. Another finely dressed gentleman ascended the steps and was given immediate entrance.

"Watch the guests." His hand slipped away from hers.

"Yes?"

"They are all men."

Another man descended from a carriage behind theirs and went into the house, this time accompanied by a delightful peal of feminine laughter.

"There are women inside," she said.

"Yet not arriving with the men." By the light of the carriage lamp his gaze was now on her. "What does that tell you?"

"That it is a gentlemen's club of some sort."

"Looks like a bawdy house for toffs," Rory offered.

"A bawdy house?" Esme said.

"A brothel," Charlie said.

"Oh." A delightful little fever ignited in her body. "But this is such an elegant address."

"Men of wealth have the same desires as lesser men, Miss Astell."

"But why would a man bring a dog to a brothel?"

"Because he has reason to fear losing it," he said grimly.

"Well, let's go."

He halted her hand again before it reached the door handle. This time he did not release it.

"No," he said.

"I will not enter the house through the front door."

"You will not enter the house at all. Rory, return Miss Astell to her boardinghouse." He put coins in the boy's palm.

"This is now my project as much as it is yours," she said. "And with two people we are much more likely to be able to steal the dog than only one person alone. It is simple mathematics."

"Not on your life."

"Rather, on yours." A heavy pain curled in her stomach.

"Esme," he said, his hand tightening around hers. "I will not put you in danger another moment."

She wrapped her free hand around his, leaned forward, and drew his scent into her nostrils.

"As your friend, Charlie, I have an obligation to you. And although you will not share with me the mystery behind this dog theft, it is clear that it is tremendously important to you. I cannot stand idly by. Anyway, I have always wanted to see the inside of a brothel."

He pulled his hand free of hers. "Esme," he ground out.

"Charlie," she replied in the same tone. "What if he has given the dog over to servants to care for while he disports himself?"

"What's *disports*?" Rory said.

"Tarries," she said.

Charlie lifted a brow.

"Frolics?"

"*Frolics?*" Rory screwed up his nose.

"Oh, bother, choose whatever word you wish," she said. "I will enter through the rear entrance and ingratiate myself with the staff. I see in your eyes that you know I can. Then I will search the backstairs while you search the front. But you won't . . ." She glanced at Rory. His attention was on another gentleman entering the house, this time greeted at the door by an attractive woman with long black hair and garbed in a flowing robe. Esme returned her attention to Charlie. "That is, you won't . . ."

His eyes glinted. He knew what she wanted to ask.

"You *won't*," she finally said.

"Frolic?" he said, a smile lifting one side of his mouth.

"Will you?"

A gleam lit his eyes. "Not unless I see something I particularly like."

"Something?" she exclaimed. "Charles Westley Brittle, you are—"

He grabbed her hand and brought it to his grinning lips.

"Remember," he said as she gaped, "these men are here for one thing. Take care."

She nodded. He released her and descended from the carriage. She craned her neck to watch him enter the house as Rory directed the driver to continue around the block. Climbing out, she asked the coachman to remain until she returned.

He shook his head. "A pretty lass like you shouldna be goin' in there, no matter Mrs. Eagan's as decent an employer as any in the trade."

"Oh, I'm sure I shall be entirely safe."

She waved at Rory still in the carriage and hurried along the alley to the rear of the house. The tradesman's door was open and she entered.

In the narrow corridor was a small group of people: one older woman in a simple starched frock and cap, one man in livery, and two young women dressed in gorgeous gowns with rouge on their lips and jewels dangling from their ears and necks. One of the gorgeously gowned women was weeping.

"You mustna cry, Peg," the older woman said, clucking her tongue. "'Tis for the health o' the bairn you be carrying."

"I *know*." Peg sniffled. "But Danny said if I dinna send the money, he'd turn out Mum an' little Dicky, an' Dicky's only just outta the workhouse an' eatin' again. I canna let me brother return there. I've to take a customer tonight, or—" She burst into tears anew.

"You shall have half of my earnings tonight," the other young woman said, her accent thickly French.

"You've your own family to feed, Aurelie," the matron said, shaking her head.

"You there." The footman was staring at Esme. "Who're you?"

All eyes came to her. As though her heartbeat weren't drumming wildly in her ears, she closed the door and went toward them.

"I am Priscilla. Mrs. Eagan sent for me." She went directly to the weeping girl. "I haven't a family and will be glad to share my earnings tonight with you, Peg." She sent up a prayer that Charlie was carrying money. He would disapprove of this hugely. But that hardly mattered now.

Peg's watery eyes were full of astonishment. "You would do this for a person you dinna ken?"

"Others have done the same for me." Gabrielle and Mineola, when she had first come to Gracechurch Street, lending her money to pay for board until her employer gave over her first month's wages. "I came on short notice tonight, however, and you see I am not suitably dressed."

The weeping girl burst into tears anew. "Thank you, miss! Thank you!"

"Now, dinna crush the gown, Peg," the matron said. "I've no' brought another tonight so she'll have to wear it."

Esme assumed the woman was a housekeeper or some such; she didn't have any idea how brothels were managed. But she went with her, along with Peg and Aurelie, a bit giddy and only slightly anxious that if Charlie had already found the dog and was on his way out of the house, she might have a very different night than she had planned.

Chapter Eight

When she entered the drawing room, Charlie thought the dim lighting was playing tricks with his vision. Or that he was hallucinating.

But there were sufficient candles to highlight the shimmer of her hair and the glimmer in her eyes, and he hadn't drunk enough to be seeing things that did not exist. That, and his body's instant reaction, told him that the beautiful woman across the chamber was indeed Esme Astell.

She wore a gown of pale blue that revealed a shadowed cleft between her breasts and clung to her hips and thighs as she moved. A string of diamonds glittered around her throat and golden tresses tumbled down her neck from an arrangement that was at once elegant and playful. Her lips were rouged, her eyes lined delicately with kohl, and her arms entirely bare save for a single strand of diamonds clasped around her upper arm.

Every man in the room was staring at her, and several of the women.

He had learned swiftly that the house was not a brothel, rather a private party hosted by a gentleman with political aspirations seeking to please potential allies.

Charlie's father had long considered public office, and he himself knew enough about how municipal politics functioned to be able to bluff his way through several conversations so far. But most of the men here tonight—and the women hired to serve them—seemed more interested in enjoying slightly risqué humor than in discussing politics.

Charlie had only one pressing need. His quarry had already gone upstairs with a woman, carrying the dog beneath his arm like a satchel.

By his behavior, it was clear Eustace Smythe-Eggers didn't care about that dog. Charlie had no idea why he wanted it. But that didn't matter. Now he just needed to get upstairs too, and he had spent the past half hour trying to imagine how he could accomplish it without taking a woman with him.

The solution stood across the room. That he was half furious with her and half insanely aroused was to be expected.

The madam was speaking softly at her shoulder, and Esme's lips curved into a slow smile. She said something to Mrs. Eagan, and the madam's gaze swept the drawing room then halted on him. The madam nodded at him.

An invitation.

He stood, crossed the room, and could feel the envious eyes of a half dozen men on him.

Up close the perfumer was even more beautiful than ever,

the candlelight making her eyes violet, and making the twinkle in them obvious. Decorated like a high-priced harlot, she was still the same Esme.

"Mr. Brittle," the madam purred. "May I present to you Miss Glorioso?"

"Good evening, Miss Glorioso." He bowed.

"Sir." Esme curtsied.

He offered his arm. She did not place her hand upon it; instead she curled her fingers snugly around his elbow and batted her lashes—but only once. A diamond comb glittered in her upswept tresses.

He drew her into the foyer.

"Lovely weather this evening," she said as they passed a couple descending the stairs. "I thought it might rain, but it has held off."

"Mm."

"What a delightfully designed stairway this is to curve so roundly," she said. "I do enjoy whimsical architecture, don't you, Mr. Brittle?"

"Mm hmm." They ascended the landing and went into the corridor.

"I read today in the—"

He pulled her into an open room and shut the door.

"Don't shout," she whispered quickly, backing up a step. "Everyone will hear."

"I have no intention of shouting."

"You don't?" Her eyes were wide, her lips parted, the pulse in her throat beating rapidly just above the diamond choker.

She was stunning.

"Of course not," he said. "And while I am not happy you are here, I don't want to hear how it happened. Not now. Now I've got to find that dog." He opened the door. Her hand on his arm was like a sudden brand, the heat of it going directly to his groin.

"You cannot go alone."

"I can. I will. Remain here."

"If anyone sees you they will wonder why you are prowling around the corridors. I should go with you."

"*Esme.*"

"Miss Glorioso," she corrected. Her lips twitched. "Isn't that the most hilarious name? I told them I was Priscilla but I think it was not glamorous enough for these jewels. They are paste, of course. You know this is not a regular broth—"

"Esme." He pinched the bridge of his nose. "I need that dog. And I need to get you out of here before any one of the wolves downstairs decides you'll be dinner tonight."

"Agreed. Entirely. But together we will find the dog quicker, and you won't be thrown out as a Peeping Tom. Come on." She brushed past him, fulfilling a favorite fantasy and sending all the blood in his body rushing into his cock. Pulling the door wide, she looked over her shoulder and pressed a single finger to her lips.

Perfect lips.

Lips that tasted like a man's fantasies.

Lips he wanted everywhere on him.

Discipline.

Control.

He dredged up every ounce of willpower that he had nurtured aboard ship to save his neck countless times when he had wanted to shout and scream that he was not supposed to be there, that it was all a hellish mistake, that he'd done nothing—*nothing*—in his life to deserve this.

But to his knowledge Esme had done nothing in her life to instantly assume a man would raise his voice to her.

He watched as she moved to the next door, the gown rippling over her buttocks like water as she moved, and his partial erection became full.

They glanced into two open bedchambers and paused at two other closed doors before he heard it. He gestured for her to halt and she came silently to his side. Just on the other side of the door, a dog was whining.

Success.

He glanced up into Esme's eyes and found them wide. And full of happiness.

His head was abruptly empty of every thought but grabbing her and doing things to her he couldn't say aloud. Things that involved her gorgeous mouth. On him.

"Don't," he whispered.

"Don't what?" Her lips formed the words without sound.

"Don't smile like that."

"Why not?" she whispered.

"When you smile like that, I—"

Her gaze snapped to the door. From within the bedchamber were now coming the unmistakable noises of a man in the throes.

"There's no more time." Charlie glanced up and down the

corridor to ensure no one watched, grasped the door handle, and drew it open two inches.

A tiny white dog hurled itself out through the crack and leaped into Charlie's arms. It was the most incongruous sight: the miniature fluffy creature scrabbling all over his broad chest with ecstatic wiggles and trying to lick his jaw.

"*Hush,*" he whispered, pulling the door silently shut, and setting the creature on the floor. It leaped about in a few speedy circles and then went tearing down the corridor only to reach the far end and come hurtling back, its tiny legs moving fast. Esme laughed and it felt so wonderfully good to release the nerves that had wound tight since she entered the drawing room.

"Why, it is as though it already knows you," she said as it pawed up his shins again, then went scampering away in joy once more.

"It does." He looked up at her. "I stole it from its owner."

"*You?*"

"I'll explain later. Now we've got to—*blast.*"

Voices were echoing in the stairwell. His gaze was on her body and little bursts of flame were heating her inside everywhere.

"What?" she said.

"Nowhere to hide it."

"My cloak is downstairs with the rest of my clothes." The voices sounded closer. "I'll—"

"There's no time." He pointed to a door that stood ajar, scooped up the dog in one hand, and tossed it in through the opening. Charlie snapped the door shut in front of her and suddenly he was behind her, crowding her against the door, his hands on her waist and his head bending over her shoulder.

He kissed her bare skin. Ecstatic tingles fanned across her flesh.

"What are you—"

"Make sounds," he whispered, his lips brushing along her shoulder. A shudder of pleasure went through her. His hands moved up the sides of her waist, sinking her in delirium.

"Sounds?" she barely managed. She had *dreamed* of this, dreamed of him holding her and touching her, so many dreams. Now he was doing it in the corridor of a stranger's house with more strangers about to appear.

"Moan," he whispered, his palms sliding over her gown, moving forward and covering her belly. His mouth shifted to her neck and his lips were hot, soft, *wonderful*, his hair tickling her chin.

"Wh-what?"

"Moan. Make noises. As though you are enjoying this."

As though.

Then she understood. Within the room, the dog was whining.

She attempted a moan. It felt good, and exactly what his caresses were making her want to do anyway. She moaned again, louder, letting it come forth naturally. His hands on her abdomen were big and strong and his lips on her neck were making a havoc of need inside her.

She heard the voices in the corridor. The conversation

halted abruptly, then started up again more softly. But Esme was hardly aware of the couple passing by. Charlie's hands had descended to her hips, and she could feel the wall of man behind her, the taut control in his body, and the brush of her tight nipples against the door panel. His hands smoothed down her thighs and her next moan was effortless.

With his fingers circling her hips, he drew her back against him.

Esme had grown up on a farm. She knew the signs of a male animal's arousal. And she knew now that the man behind her was aroused.

In for a penny . . .

Pressing her hips back, she rubbed against him.

"*Esme.*" The single word was uttered harshly. But he did not push her away. Instead he pulled her more snugly to him.

"Do you like this?" she whispered with a quiver in her voice.

"Yes." The word came as a reverberation against her back. Then his hand slid down her belly and between her legs.

She gasped, moaned, made all sorts of other sounds that covered up the dog's whine.

"You?" he said against her neck, his teeth grazing her jaw and sending spirals of need down to where his hand was touching her.

"Yes," she panted. "*Yes.*" She let him stroke his fingers over her and groaned again, harder. It was sublimely sweet and sharp, weakening and delicious and perfect and she wanted more. She was *wild* for more. Something within her was opening up, stretching, and deliriously needy. The other couple had disappeared into a bedchamber, but she never wanted this to end.

"I didn't know it was possible to feel this," he whispered, his other hand moving up her stomach and to the base of her breast, circling her ribs as though to hold her in place. The stroking had become massage between her legs and she throbbed there with a furiously needy ache.

"Silk in a brothel?" she whispered, trying to remain rational.

"Victorious and satisfied," he said, his thumb stroking the underside of her breast as his hand continued the caress between her thighs and her breaths disappeared entirely. "And hungry. All at once."

She swiveled around in his arms. With a sound in his chest that might have been a protest or a groan, he bent his head and captured her mouth beneath his.

It was no tentative kiss, no first or chaste or hesitant meeting of lips, but deep and lustful and hungry. Esme had been kissed before, but not like this—not like he knew her mouth better than she did, knew every tender place and knew how the caress of his tongue could spike in her the urge to spread her thighs and take him between them. She could feel his hunger yet there was no haste, only depth and his scent and another, stronger scent twining all through her: lust, the musky mingling of two animals that wanted to mate—that *needed* it.

His hands were in her hair and his body was so hard, his strength thoroughly devoted to her, and his mouth consuming her lips and tongue. *Kissing* her. Charles Brittle kissing *her* as though he could not get enough of her. It made her weak and ecstatic, and she was certain, *certain*, that if she offered him more he would take it.

Welcoming his lips on her jaw, then her throat, she pulled in lungfuls of air, shuddering, loving his kiss, this caress she probably should not be allowing—but if not now, then when, or ever? As though in a dream she allowed her knees to part. With a groan, he accepted the invitation, bringing his body against her as he took her mouth again, and bore her up against the door.

It was unreal. It was heaven—such powerful *feeling*, such breathless rightness. He was hard between her thighs, rocking to her as their lips fed on each other's desire.

But the dog was whining, a pitiful whimper of abandonment.

She wrested her mouth from beneath his.

"Should we leave?" she said, panting a little.

His hands ran up and down her sides.

"Esme," he said very low and rough. His gaze swept over her face. "We've got to leave."

"Do you have any money?"

The beautiful hazel eyes were bewildered. "Money?"

"How much do you imagine it costs to hire a—that is— me?"

"*What?*" He broke away from her. "Esme—"

"No, no, it's not what you think! Only give me half of what it would cost to hire me for tonight. Now. Please. But . . . do you know how much it would cost?"

His throat moved in an awkward swallow. He nodded.

A sick little twist of nerves wriggled through her stomach. "Please give it to me. The money."

He reached into his pocket and pulled out bills.

She stared. "Good heavens, that much? I suppose it is an entire night."

His chest was moving hard. "For an hour."

"An *hour?*"

"For you, yes." There was a gleam in his eyes. Definitely wolfish.

From brow to toes she was feverish. Snatching the money from his hand, she went before him toward the servants' stairwell and heard him open the door; the dog yipped in delight.

She found Peg and the older woman, and tucked the money into Peg's palm.

Peg gaped.

"If you ever need a friend or help," Esme said, squeezing her hands, "write to Esme Astell at Skinner's Perfumery in London. I will return the gown and jewelry tomorrow."

They stared at Charlie as he touched his hand to her lower back and ushered her out the door.

As they ran down the mews alley there was no sound but the pattering of their footsteps. A minute later he was opening the carriage door and ordering Rory out of it.

"Find all the boys," he said as he handed her up and passed the dog to her. "Then meet me at the Thistle at midnight."

"Aye, aye, sir." Rory ran off into the night.

Charlie gave the coachman an address, climbed in, and closed the door. The dog leaped onto his lap and he gave its ears a ruffle with his fingers, then set it on the seat beside Esme, where it curled up in a happy little ball and watched him.

"Why did you give that girl the money?" he said.

"She was supposed to work tonight. But it seems that she is increasing, and the madam would not allow it, and— What? You look odd. Is this the right dog after all?"

"You could have been—" He ran his hand over his face, then into his hair. "You could have been hurt."

"I knew you were there."

"I might have already left."

"Then I would have escaped. Somehow. Charlie, what are you worrying about? I am here, safe, and we have the dog! Now you will tell me how it is you came to steal it and who is the man who had it and what you plan to do with it now."

"A man named Pate holds the promissory note on my life."

"Promissory note? On your *life?*"

"I owe him money. Owed. I didn't have it. He wanted this animal, apparently to pay a debt to Smythe-Eggers, the man at that party back there. Pate said if I got the dog for him he would wipe my slate clean."

"Wipe your slate clean? What on earth does that *mean?*"

"He owns my life. As a member of his crew, I am a captive. Unless I pay him his price, he will hunt me down and kill me as a message to others in his service."

"I—I see." She drew a slow breath to steady her nerves. "Why have you stolen back the dog tonight?"

"Because it was wrong to steal it."

"It was wrong?"

"Of course."

"But your *life*—What if Pate discovers you are returning it to its owner? I suppose that is your intention?"

His features relaxed as he glanced at the dog. It was immobile, exhausted after its ordeal, but its eyes were fixed on him.

"Yes," he said. "By the time Pate discovers it—not *if*, for he will discover it—I will be gone."

A tight knot wound itself about her stomach.

Charlie lifted his gaze to hers and she forgot about the dog and villains and that he was leaving imminently. There was such heat in his eyes.

"Esme," he said deeply. "Back there, in the house, when we—"

Then she was across the carriage and on his lap and twining her hands through his hair as he wrapped his arms around her. Their mouths met, retreated, met again, then connected so deeply Esme moaned.

"I said I would not throw myself at you," she said amidst his onslaught of kisses.

"I really wanted you to," he said in a rumbling growl and his hands were all over her, spread down her back, then tucking around her buttocks and pulling her to him.

The silky fabric of her gown and undergarments gave way easily to his hands. The heat of his palms and fingers on her bared legs made her arch to him and meet his tongue with hers. She was aching so powerfully, the place between her legs so hungry for his hand again. She had long known how animals came together. But the throbbing, needy heat in her body was showing her why any of them bothered. His hands were completing the education. With his palm between her thighs, his thumb was stroking her skin.

Then he touched her—intimately. With nothing between his skin and her flesh, it was a revelation. Pure beauty.

A caress. A flick of the tip of his thumb. Another caress.

She moaned, writhed on his lap, desperately hungry for his mouth as she pulled at her skirts, dragging them out from beneath her and finding his hips with her knees, straddling him and kissing him deeper. There weren't enough kisses in the world. He was still touching her there, still making her wild with need. Trapping his hand between their bodies, she rocked to his arousal.

"*Esme,*" he groaned, and pressed his finger into her. She shuddered at the sensation. He was stroking her *and* penetrating her and it was *too good.* She was mad for it. With each indulgent thrust of his finger her thighs opened wider. "Esme." Delectable and perfect, each thrust, each caress made the ache even sweeter and tighter. She was whimpering, pushing to him, desperate for even more, wanting, *needing*—

The carriage jolted through a pothole and came to an abrupt halt.

Removing his hand from between them and reaching up to smooth her hair back, he took her face between his palms and brought their mouths together. He kissed her and then again, then again, as though he would not cease or at least did not want to cease.

"Irresistible." His hands slipped down her back. "You are perfectly irresistible."

She loved the sensation of his hard arms beneath her hands.

"You needn't resist." The husky quality of her words surprised her.

"Yet I must."

"You must return the dog now," she said, feeling his chest with her palms and wondering that she was straddling his lap and had been mere moments from giving herself to him entirely. She still wanted to.

"Yes."

She could see nothing of him, but his voice sounded peculiarly raw.

"And then leave town," she said. "That is, leave the continent."

"Yes."

"All right," she said and took a deep breath. She climbed off him and straightened her skirts and sat back. "Go return the dog, Mr. Brittle."

When, dog cradled to his chest, he had descended from the carriage and closed the door, she opened the curtain and peered out. Without street lamps, the full moon illuminated a house set not far from others, cottage-like and exceedingly modest. There were pots of winter greenery on the stoop and the porch was clean of debris.

He disappeared around the side of the house, and was gone for only a few minutes. When he reappeared he had no dog.

He sat beside her in the carriage.

"You do not intend to make love to me now," she said.

"No." In the moonlight she could see his slight smile. The carriage jerked into movement.

"It is for the best that we were interrupted," she said.

"It is."

When they arrived at the boardinghouse he dismissed the coach and watched her hike up her skirts so she could get her first foothold on the way to her bedchamber window.

"This gown is narrower than mine." She struggled with it.

He came to her, took her hand, and, ducking to draw her arm over his head, turned his back to her.

"You will not carry me up on your back!"

"Are you doubting my strength?"

"No. That is, I—"

"It's this or remove the gown," he said. "Or you could come home with me." His voice sent a spark of perfect delight up her center.

"Do you have a home?"

"Not at present, actually. But I do have a bed."

"Charles Westley Brittle—"

"You always use my full name before you chastise me. I like it." He was smiling. "And I like it now especially, since chastising me for this after—"

"Oh, hush." She slung her arms about his neck and held

on tight as he climbed. When they reached the window he let her clamber over him and into the room. By the time she twisted around and got her feet beneath her, he was gone.

For quite some time she sat on the floor in the cool night air and thought of his kiss and his delectably intimate touch and how he had not, again, said goodbye before disappearing forever.

CHAPTER NINE

The Blue Thistle
Port of Leith, Scotland

Charlie was sitting at a table at the rear of the Blue Thistle, both hands around a pint he was not drinking, when the man who had made his life a living hell for nearly two years strode through the door.

Having learned a thing or two from the pirate captain during that time, he did not spring up and look about to ensure Rory's safety. Instead he remained seated but removed one of his hands from the glass, making ready to grab his dagger.

"Where's the boy?" Pate grumbled. He was a bear of a man, shorter than Charlie by inches but stout as a barrel. Charlie had discovered early in their acquaintance that the barrel was entirely comprised of muscle. Robert Pate had not reached nearly six decades by being soft in any manner.

"The boy?" Charlie said, lifting the pint to his mouth. He'd no desire to drink, only to appear unconcerned.

"The boy who's been running about town at your bidding."

"I've no idea." Which was true. After meeting the boys here two nights ago, knowing Pate would return soon he had told them to disappear for a bit.

Pate lowered his heft onto a chair.

"I'll have that money now, Scholar," he said calmly, as though a fortnight earlier he had not said that unless Charlie gave over three hundred pounds or stole the dog he would string him up from a yardarm and watch him swing.

"I delivered the dog to you, yet you set the police on me," Charlie said just as evenly. "That was not part of our bargain, Pate."

"Neither was snatching the dog from Smythe-Eggers."

The barkeep set a bottle and a glass on the table. Charlie watched the pirate pour a dram and throw it back.

"Why does Smythe-Eggers want the dog? He looks well-heeled enough to purchase his own."

Pate shook his head slowly.

"You've much yet to learn, lad. I've told you a hundred times, a man's desires are two: power and pleasure."

"The old woman's poor as a church mouse. What could Smythe-Eggers want from her?"

"The pile of gold she's sitting on."

"There is buried treasure on her property?"

"Of a sort."

"How would stealing the dog—" But Charlie already knew. In the days since he had taken Douglass from Mrs. Wallis's house, her health had declined swiftly. Two nights earlier, looking down on her sleeping, he had seen her wan cheeks and the bones protruding from her hands, and knew that the animal was her only joy. As he had deposited the dog on the floor and it leaped up onto the bed to snuggle beside her, he had resigned himself to this moment—now, here, his life again in Pate's hands.

"Why'd you do it, lad?" Shaking his head, Pate seemed suddenly weary. "Why'd you go and nab that dog again? That pink-faced runt Smythe-Eggers is spitting mad. Now I've to pay him the money I owe him, and you know I don't like sharing me gold with namby-pambies."

"It is of no interest to me, Pate, what you like or dislike. I did what you wished: I stole the dog and delivered it to you. I am no longer required to listen to your rules or preferences or dislikes." He set a coin on the table for the drink and stood up.

Pate released a histrionic sigh.

"Guess I'll have to ask the girl where the dog's gone," he mumbled as though to himself.

Charlie rounded on him.

Pate rose, standing to his full height and Charlie forced his breaths to come slowly. He wasn't the cowardly shopkeeper that Pate had dragged onto his ship, tortured into submission, then trained to villainy. With the threat to her in his ears, now he felt invincible.

"You go near her, Pate, and I will kill you. I will turn every skill you taught me, and the skills I acquired on my own, to that purpose alone."

Pate's salty whiskers creased into a wide grin. "There's my boy. I said I'd make a man out of you, and look here, I have." He moved toward the door. "Tomorrow, Scholar, you bring me that dog or the money, or I find that pretty bit of muslin and I turn her world upside down."

"God damn you, P—"

"I won't touch her." The pirate looked around at him. "Ever seen me harm a hair on the head of a female?"

Charlie hadn't. But it was small comfort.

"No," Pate said. "But I'll ruin her nonetheless. Don't doubt me. I'm a man of my word, Scholar. You know that too."

How it was possible to be at once heartbroken and euphoric, Esme could not fathom. But she was.

Monsieur Cadence, with typical Gallic sensitivity, seemed to know. On the penultimate day of the meeting, after several sessions that filled her head with new ideas while her heart was trying its best to continue beating regularly, he invited her to take an aperitif before returning to the boardinghouse.

"I have heard the rumor, mademoiselle, that gives me at once great happiness and great sorrow," he said, sipping his wine and watching the passersby. The evening was mild, and people of all sorts were strolling along the footpath.

"Oh, no," she said. "I wish it were only happiness."

"Yet I must be glad for this sorrow. For I have heard a little bird say that our friend Pierre will invite you to Paris."

"Monsieur Poe intends to invite *me?*"

Monsieur Cadence raised his glass. "To Mademoiselle Astell, the finest young perfumer in all the lands."

Bidding him goodnight, she walked the length of Old Town back to the boardinghouse. Not allowing her gaze to stray to the Hart and Rose and bypassing the alley in which he had taught her to climb up the side of a building, she went inside and requested her key.

"I've let the room, lass," the boardinghouse proprietress said with customary irritability.

Esme blinked. "You've let my room?"

"Aye. Now dinna be crowdin' up my foyer. Off with you."

"Mrs. McDade, how could you have let my room?" Panic stole beneath her skin. "I paid the full ten days in advance." And now had only enough to pay for the coach fare back to London. "I have two more nights in that room."

"'Tis let, missy, an' I'll no' hear another word."

"But—"

"They left this for you." Mrs. McDade tossed a letter on the desk.

"They?"

"The niffy-naffs that carried away your luggage."

"My *luggage?*" She took up the letter. On thick creamy paper—the sort Charlie had always kept in a box on his desk at Brittle and Sons—the letter bore her name in scrolling calligraphy.

Inside was only a calling card for the manager of a hotel in New Town, the gloriously elegant establishment she had shown Charlie days earlier.

"'The men who took my luggage left this?" she said to Mrs. McDade.

"Aye. Now be off with you, lass. I've a business to run here."

In bemusement, Esme again walked across town, the sun setting beautifully over the hills to the west and casting dramatic shadows everywhere. The scents of cooking came on the evening breeze and the sounds of laughter and chatter wafted from the doorways of pubs.

Inside the rose and ivory splendor of the hotel's main foyer, an elegantly dressed man approached.

"Miss Astell, I presume?" he said.

"Why—yes. How do you know my name?"

"I was given a precise description o' you. I am the manager here. I will show you to your room."

"Oh. But I have only come for my luggage, which it seems was mistakenly delivered here."

"It was not mistakenly delivered, Miss Astell," he said. "You are to stay with us for the next two days."

"I am? But I've no—that is to say, I cannot afford a room in your hotel. I cannot afford a cup of tea in your hotel." She laughed.

"Your room and meals have already been paid for. Now, if you will, I shall show you to your room."

She followed him, wondering if Monsieur Poe had arranged this. Perhaps awaiting her in the room would be an invitation to join him in Paris.

There was no invitation, only a large bedchamber of

sumptuous comfort. A thick rug was soft beneath her tired feet, the walls were wainscoted and white, the mantel over the fireplace was ivory marble, and the bedclothes were creamy white and embroidered with rosebuds. A vase of white and pink roses filled the space with sweet scent. Her small traveling trunk was set on a stand. And on a table, laid out in creamy china, was a feast of apples, cheese, roasted pheasant, custards, biscuits, and wine fit for a king.

"This is beautiful!" She turned to the manager. "Are you certain it is for *me?*"

"Quite certain, miss."

"Did Monsieur Poe arrange it? Or Monsieur Cadence, perhaps?"

"The gentleman did not offer his name. But he was most certainly English, and his manners were impeccable. Now I will leave you to your dinner. If you should require anything, simply ring the bell."

Alone, sitting on the edge of the bed, she clasped her hands together to still their trembling.

Charlie had done this—Charlie, who had kissed and touched her within an inch of making love to her, then simply disappeared. Again.

Yet . . . *this.*

Falling back on the mattress and into decadent feather down, she laughed and wept a little and then laughed again. It was no wonder that she had loved him for years.

Drying her cheeks, she washed her hands and face in the

basin of water kept warm on a washstand beside the fireplace, then poured wine into a crystal goblet and took it to the window. From this height, she could see all the way over to the castle in Old Town. Dipping her gaze to the street below, she almost dropped the glass.

He stood across the street, leaning against the wall and looking directly up at her.

Her pirate.

Snatching up her cloak, she dashed out of the room, down the stairs, and out the door.

As she neared him, he smiled.

"How is it?" he said.

"Gorgeous." She wanted to throw her arms around him and kiss his smiling lips. "Why did you do it?"

"To thank you."

"But you said days ago that you haven't any money."

"I found some."

She lifted a brow. "Stole some?"

"Not this time."

"You did not give your name to the manager. If you meant to be mysterious, why are you here now?"

"I came to say goodbye."

A mote of hope—hope that he had not said goodbye the other night because he had not yet left Edinburgh and still meant to see her—had remained in Esme, until this moment.

"I imagined you already en route to Boston," she said.

"Not yet. Would you care for a stroll, Miss Astell?" He offered his arm.

Obviously he did not understand that she had spent the past forty-eight hours trying to rid her mind, heart, and body of the memories of touching him.

"Thank you, sir." She tucked her fingers around his elbow and he tightened his arm to his side.

They strolled and she spoke of her admiration of the buildings, the elegant square that seemed still to be under construction, the magnificent carriages, a gentleman's ivory-tipped walking cane, a lady's lacy parasol, and anything else that would allow her to continue speaking so that they could avoid the goodbye she dreaded. The early-spring evening was all around them in budding leaves and rain-dampened cobbles, but she barely smelled it. She did not remove her hand from his arm and he held her firmly there. It was intoxicating and maddening to be at once so close and yet not closer.

By the time they again stood in the great hall of the hotel, she was gripping his sleeve so tightly that her fingertips ached.

"May I escort you to your door?" he said rather formally.

"Thank you, sir."

As they ascended the stairs, her mouth continued its attempt at denial of what would come momentarily with a continuous catalogue of the hotel's accoutrements. In murmurs he agreed with her praise of the elegant risers, the paintings adorning the walls, and the chandelier that illumined all. But when she glanced aside, he was not looking at them; he seemed to be studying the tips of his boots with great sobriety.

Arriving before the door to her room, he lifted her hand to his lips.

"Miss Astell, this must be goodb—"

"There is an impressive dinner laid out inside. Would you care to share it with me? You paid for it, after all."

His grip tightened about her hand.

Finally she lifted her gaze to his eyes that she had not met in an hour. What she saw there tore the breath from her lungs.

"That would be a bad idea," he said, his voice very low and marvelously rough.

"The best bad idea ever."

His chest rose and fell upon a hard breath.

Upon her own stumbling heartbeat, she found herself nodding. And then, as though longing were a quality one could taste in the air, it passed between them, and pure, honest desire.

Seizing her about the waist, he swung her into her room, kicked the door shut, and dragged her into his arms. Their mouths met, her fingers sank into his hair, and his hands flattened her body to his.

"I am leaving," he said and kissed her again.

"I know." She pressed herself more tightly to him and could not kiss him fast enough, close enough.

"Leaving Scotland." His hands moved over her back, up and then down, his palms exploring her hips and making her weak with need. "Britain."

"I know."

"I *cannot* do this," he said, seizing her face between his

hands as though he would force her away, and instead kissing her once, twice, again, each time more closely.

"You can," she said. "We can."

His hands descended again, now to her waist, pulling her yet tighter against him, and she felt every glorious part of his body against hers.

"Esme, I—"

She pressed two fingertips to his lips. Sliding them down his chin and throat, she felt the jerk of his Adam's apple.

"Don't speak. Don't say anything." She lifted her gaze to his. The beautiful gray-green of his eyes was unfocused, fevered.

"Please," she whispered.

There was no asking again. No begging. No making plain to him in further words what was perfectly plain in her hands that clutched his shoulders as he released the fasteners of her gown, and equally obvious in her lips as she explored the rough texture of his jaw. Then he was sweeping away her gown and she was before him in her petticoat and his hands were curving up her waist and around the sides of her breasts.

"Beautiful," he said so deeply she barely heard it above the pounding of her heart. "Perfectly beautiful," he said and as his hands covered her breasts he bent his head and took her neck with his mouth.

Nothing she had felt before, not even with him in the carriage, had prepared her for the shower of pleasure across her skin, delving beneath the surface and fanning everywhere. Through the linen his fingers found the edge of her shift, and then beneath it her nipples, taut and aching to be touched.

He touched them, generously, his lips on the sensitive skin of her neck making each pass of his fingertips a current of beauty running between them, until it was almost unbearable.

Then she opened his mouth on her and she could not remain still. With shaking fingers she tore at the buttons of his waistcoat, then pushed it over his shoulders, coat and all. His hands returned to her petticoat, unlacing now, and her stays; to the floor they went too. Grabbing his waist, she tugged his shirt and pulled it up. He took the tails in his hands and its removal over his head was a thing of beauty, each muscle in his chest and waist rippling beneath taut golden skin, sending heat pulsing between her thighs. Her gaze swept up a flat abdomen to the contours above. And abruptly halted in shock.

"Char—"

He pulled her to him and his mouth covered hers. She allowed it, held his face in her hands and felt him through only the thin linen of her shift.

Then she broke away, grabbed his wrists, and stared.

"What—what is—" She could not continue. Spiraling from his forearms to his shoulders were images of ropes so perfectly rendered in black ink that they seemed to sit upon the surface of his skin. She ran her fingertips over the stains, across the thick veins in his forearms and up the swirling twine that mounted the rounded muscle of his upper arms and curled over his shoulders.

"What are they?" she whispered, feeling only the taut heat of his skin beneath her hands.

"My bonds," he said. "The permanent proof that I am no longer a gentleman."

"Who did this to you?"

"A man who did not care for my ability to talk circles around him. Does it repel you?"

Wrenching her attention from the ropes, she looked into eyes that were again like stone. Curving her palms around his shoulders, she moved close, lifted her face, and whispered, "I am not a maiden."

He blinked.

"Does it repel you?" she said.

He kissed her. Then he kissed her again. Then again. Shortly the thin layer of linen that separated her from him was gone, and soon after their shoes and stockings as well. Skin against skin, they reveled in the flavor of kisses.

He lifted her up in his powerful ink-stained arms and carried her to the bed. Laying her on her back upon the covers of soft white cotton, he lowered himself above her.

"I have never been carried anywhere before," she whispered as his gaze moved from each of her features to the next, then down her neck to her breasts.

"How did you enjoy it?" he murmured, bending his head to feather kisses over the base of her throat, then the curve of her breast.

"Quite a lot," she said on a quivering sigh.

Then he took her nipple into his mouth and she was unable to say anything more, only to make sounds of flagrant rapture. It was divine pleasure and certainly immodest, and she did not care. His hand circled her other breast, his fingers played with the excruciatingly tight peak, and quite suddenly she wanted nothing but this for the remainder of her days, for as many days as that lasted.

Yet when his hand began a southward exploration over her belly, it turned out she wanted that too. And when his fingers slid between her thighs and found the pulse of her need, and began the maddening massage that made her arch her back and make whimpering sounds, she decided she wanted that quite fervently too.

"I could give pleasure to you," he murmured, "to this body," he said and grazed his teeth across her nipple, "forever."

Wanting to shout, "*Yes! Do! Please!*" she could only moan. A wave of tight, hard ecstasy was swallowing her, slowly, inexorably, pulling her under. It broke in thick, hot convulsions that swept up and outward. She did shout, wordlessly, gasping for breaths then crying aloud again.

His mouth left her breast and she was abruptly aware—breathlessly—of the heat of his skin between her thighs, of hard muscle urging her legs apart, then an entirely new and staggering touch.

As though he had all the time in the world and she had not just become an undulating voluptuary beneath him, he brushed the pad of his thumb across her nipple as he shifted between her thighs and sent her deep into pleasure anew, and then into further stammering convulsions.

When her high-pitched moans had quieted, his lips came to hers.

"Yes?" he asked and his voice sounded wonderfully fierce.

"Yes. Have me now."

"Have you?"

"Take me."

"*Take* you?" Now he was smiling. "To where?"

"To *heaven.*" Laughter tumbled from her. "Charles Westley Brittle, for pity's sa—Oh, *yes.*"

Their groans mingled as he fit their bodies together. It was hot and wet and thoroughly perfect, and actually heaven. No one teased now.

"Esme." He moved in her. "Esme." Stroking slowly, he uttered her name again, low and ragged in his chest where she felt it vibrate. Taut and thick and stretching her delectably he thrust again, then again, then again harder. *"Esme."* Then he was repeating her name, taking her, truly taking her, making her need him deeper, and deeper, and faster. Grasping her knee he pulled it up to hug his side, the ropes on his arms twisting, blurring as he thrust and the pleasure crested again.

She heard him call her name, heard her own cries, and then she was shaking—shaking so hard that he was gathering her in his arms as though he would prevent her from shaking to pieces, and murmuring her name into her hair again and again.

"Sweet Esme," he whispered hoarsely. "Sweet, sweet, beautiful Esme." His lips strafed her brow, then the bridge of her nose, then her temple and cheek and finally her mouth. "Are you—"

"Perfect" shot from her lips upon very little air. "Perfect. Oh, *so* perfect. That was—it was *perfect*." She opened her eyes. "Shall we do it again? Let's."

Creases formed on either side of his mouth. He closed the space between their lips and she locked her arms about his neck as he demonstrated once again how superbly well their mouths fit together too.

But, however absolutely delightful it was to run her fingers through the short hair at the nape of his neck, she was unsatisfied with that exploration alone. Smoothing her palms downward, she let them experience the gloriously firm expanse of his shoulders and then—

Her breaths caught between a sigh of pleasure at the sensation of smooth skin over taut muscle, and a gasp of horror at the sensation of something quite different.

Her hands stilled.

He lifted his head.

"Aha," he said as though he were only discovering the scars beneath her fingers now too.

"Charlie—"

"The catalogue of my imperfections is as dull as it is lengthy," he said, brushing his wonderful lips across hers again and then gently drawing away. "I would much rather quiz you on the—shall we say?—discarding of your maidenhood."

Settling on his side along the length of her, elbow propped beneath him, he was looking at her, really studying her, his gaze traveling over her face and then her breasts and then trailing down her belly. Everywhere his gaze touched her skin felt aflame, hovering somewhere between lust for the raw virility stretched out for her viewing enjoyment and very silly embarrassment. She had not, after all, ever been entirely naked with another person. Now, however, she found that she liked being naked with *him*. Quite a lot.

"So?" he said.

"It is not a particularly interesting story."

He smiled slightly. "Dull and lengthy too?"

"Painful and brief, rather," she said.

Anger sparked in his eyes. "Painful?"

"Oh, no," she said swiftly. "Not—that is—I was willing. Entirely. But it was, well, a mistake."

Now his brow knit. "A mistake?"

She nodded.

"Esme, men don't make *mistakes*. Not of that sort."

"Perhaps *mistake* is not the correct word," she admitted. "Rather, an experiment. The boy was part of a traveling theater troupe. He was young. I was too. We were each curious and the opportunity—well, it occurred."

"I see," he said.

"You are pensive." She shifted away. "I know of course that girls should not have those sorts of desires, or women either. But my mother said it was her curse and that she passed it on to me as well."

"Curse?"

"The curse of inordinate female lustfulness, she called it. That is what a priest once said to her in the confessional. But I told her it is simply that the women in our family have particularly acute senses."

He met her gaze.

"Now you are repelled," she said.

"In fact I am wishing I had been that boy."

Her lashes did several quick flutters. "You are?"

Charlie leaned down and touched his lips to hers, which were still blowsy from his kisses.

"I would have quit the theater troupe," he said and took her cheek into his hand. Her hair was like silk where it had escaped the tight braids about her ears, soft against his fingertips.

"Would you have?" she said, her eyes half closed now and her lips almost smiling as he set his mouth to her throat and breathed in her scent of vanilla. *Vanilla.* He had not expected it. But of course the woman who could recognize every scent on the earth, each flower and herb and costly cologne, would adorn herself with such simplicity. "And survived on what income, exactly?" she said.

"Whatever came to hand," he replied promptly, tasting the sultry, salty flavor of her skin. "But I am a London boy, born and bred. What does one do to make a living in the wilds of Yorkshire—when one tends toward bookishness, that is?"

"Shear sheep. Cut crops. Dig ditches." Her smile was wide, her voice light. The caress of her fingertips skimming his arm was getting him hard again.

He lifted his head.

"I would have dug ditches to be with you, Esme Astell."

Her lips parted and for the length of five full heartbeats she was silent.

"Let's do it again," she whispered.

She was *perfect*.

"If you will finally loose these tresses from their bind-ings," he said, tracing a braid with a single finger, "we can do it as many times as you wish."

With alacrity, she loosed the tresses. Rather, together they did. To gain access to the final braid she sat up, thus revealing the beauty of her breasts and waist in a whole new posture and momentarily rendering Charlie paralyzed. She spoke to him—said something—asked him something, he thought—but he could only nod and stutter unintelligible syllables.

Not, however, for long.

Taking the laughing little beauty into his arms, he re-minded her with carefully placed kisses and caresses that lovemaking was a very serious matter indeed. Shortly she was sighing and gasping and moaning again, as she had been when he'd had her beneath him.

When the pale golden locks flowed freely about her shoulders, down her back, and over the dusky tips of her breasts, it was not outside the realm of honesty to say that he lost himself in them, in her, in thorough mutual hedonism.

Some time later—quite a lot of time later, although it seemed to both of them one continuous enchanted moment—on his back, with the golden tresses draped over his chest like a lavish blanket as she dropped kisses one after another onto his belly and her hands explored, he did not hear himself whisper between groans, "This must be a dream." Afterward, however, she told him that he had.

"Did I?" he murmured, on the cusp of sleep and trying not to tip into the abyss. As long as he remained awake, he reasoned, the dawn would not come.

"What dream?" Her fingertips were painting a portrait upon his chest, of what he hadn't any idea, but he was highly appreciative of her art.

"Every dream I have ever had," he heard himself say, knew he should not have, but refused to regret it.

"What is this scar?" she said, running a single fingertip over his shoulder.

"Musket . . . shot," he mumbled, tilting over the precipice of slumber.

"I did not tell you the truth when I said I cannot describe a person's unique scent," he thought she said, but he was dreaming already, wishes and hopes and visions of heaven just out of reach, as ever. A pirate could never bed a princess, after all. Rather, *wed*. In any case, *have*. She could never be his. Not beyond the dawn that was, he suspected, shortly to break.

"Chestnuts, warmth, and the color of burgundy wine," she whispered. "That is your scent, Charles Westley Brittle."

"Color?" Perhaps he only mouthed the words. Colors could not, after all, be scents. He thought.

She chuckled: a smooth, sweet sound of sage. *Aha*: herbs could have sounds. He was mad. And dreaming.

"I have known it since the day we met." Her fingertips stole across his lips. "Chestnuts." The tip of her tongue traced his lower lip. He struggled to open his eyes but clouds held them closed. He had not slept in days, not deeply, not in weeks. *Months.*

"Warmth." Her breath skittered across his jaw, then trailed down his neck. "And the color," she whispered against his breastbone, "of burgundy." Her tongue lapped his nipple.

Abruptly, he was fully awake and on the way to being fully aroused as well.

Grasping her shoulders, he turned her onto her back and rose above her.

Her eyes were very, very wide. Startled.

"I thought you were asleep," she said.

"Your clever tongue woke me."

"The scars on your back," she said. "They are scars from lashings."

"They are."

"Make love to me," she said, and her breasts rose and fell in quick, sharp breaths.

He did as she requested. As before, she was easily roused, and as before he was easily lost. But not so lost that he forgot his dream, or perhaps not a dream after all.

"Chestnuts, warmth, and the color of burgundy?" he said finally, when she was panting, whimpering, and begging with her body for gratification.

A pink flush suffused her cheeks and neck all the way to the tight peaks of her breasts, and her skin glistened in candlelight. Eyes closed, she turned her face away. He ducked his head and tasted the column of neck she exposed, then her breasts, then her sex that was wet and ready for him.

After that there was no further conversation, no more confessions or even laughter, only caresses.

Eventually, they slept for a short time.

As dawn crept into the sky he said goodbye—this time permanently—at the door of her room. He kissed her lips tenderly, lingering and kissing her again just as beautifully, then releasing her hands and whispering, "Goodbye, Esme."

She could not say goodbye, and could not watch him walk away. Instead she closed the door, went to the bed that was thoroughly tousled, curled up in the covers that smelled of him and of their lovemaking, and watched the dawn gradually transform into day.

CHAPTER TEN

Esme was listening to her idol pontificate about a fragrance he called Aqua d'Or—that she privately thought shouted of dandelion extract and which was an unfortunate piss-yellow color—when she realized the scratching sound she had been trying to ignore included her name. Turning her head to the rear of the room, she saw Rory's face in the window, and behind him, three of his cohorts.

He opened his mouth. She shook her head quickly. Darting glances about the lecture hall, she rose from her seat and hurried out.

Rory and the boys met her at the building's front entrance.

"Why are you here?"

"Scholar'd told us where to find you, o' course," Rory said with a crinkle in his brow that suggested she was a dimwit. "He said as we were s'posed to check in to be certain you be all right, an' that Pate weren't threatening you any." He was speaking so swiftly she could hardly decipher the words. "I'd a' come later anyway, but, miss, he's gone an' done a thing he shouldna, an' now Pate'll take him an' we've got to get that dug back an' save him an' the books, miss!"

"But—What books? I don't understand. Please explain it clearly."

"That ol' varmint Pate gave Scholar two choices: get the dug for him or pay him three hundred guineas. But Pate's found out Scholar stole the dug back again, an' now he's out for Scholar's blood."

"For—for his—" She could hardly draw breath. "For what reason did he insist on one or the other choice?"

"For Scholar's freedom from the yoke, miss! You see, Scholar'd been savin' up his gold from all the takes to buy a pile o' moldy books at an auction up at some old dead toff's mansion yesterday. O' course I asked Scholar what he'd want with old books." His eyes widened. "An' listen to what he says: he says, Rory, my boy, those books are worth far more than three hundred guineas; a man's just got to find the right buyer for each o' them an' he'll make a fortune."

Books. Antique books, by the sound of it. She had no doubt Charlie wanted the books simply because he loved working with them, and not only for the money he could make from them.

"Did he purchase them at the auction, then?"

"There be the tragedy, miss! Pate came around the Thistle yesterday sayin' he'd have Scholar back in the bilge if he dinna hand over the money or the dug. The daftie gave him the money!"

"Oh, *no.*"

"I've a suspicion he did it to put Pate off *your* scent."

"*My* scent? But how does Mr. Pate know anything about me?"

"*Ronnie*," Rory spat out. "Squealed like a stuck pig, he did."

"Oh, that is awful," she said to all four boys. "When you trusted each other like brothers. I am so sorry he betrayed you."

Rory's face split into a grin. "You're a right good 'un, miss! 'Tis the reason we've come here. You've got to help us find that dug an' save Scholar's hide."

"But I don't know how we went to the place where he left the dog. I have no idea where it is. Perhaps the hackney coach driver might remember. But there must be dozens of hackney coach drivers in this city."

"*Ils sont vingt-deux*" came just behind her.

She swung around to see Monsieur Cadence's thoughtful face.

"There are twenty-two hackney coaches in Edinburgh?" she said.

"*Oui*, mademoiselle. As I make at least one journey to this city each year, I have an investment in one of the coaches, so that I needn't ride in a filthy equipage," he said, the crinkles about his eyes deepening.

"Monsieur, these boys and I must save a dear friend." The man she still loved, despite her head telling her she mustn't. "Would you help us?"

"*Mais bien sûr*," he said with a smile. "Now tell me all."

Monsieur Cadence's coach was summoned, and the coachman consulted. The coachman who had driven her and Charlie several nights earlier was swiftly found enjoying lunch at the hackney drivers' favorite pub.

Esme missed the final afternoon of the Society's meeting. But during the drive into the countryside the Frenchman regaled the boys with stories of his travels throughout the world in search of the finest fragrances.

When they arrived at the little cottage she discovered it to be shabbier than she had noticed in the dark. The boys remained with the coach while Monsieur Cadence and she went to the door.

An ancient woman answered. The tiny dog at her ankles took one sniff of Esme and began racing in circles while emitting ecstatic yips and yelps.

The woman peered at them. "How may I help you?"

"Madam," the Frenchman said with a deep bow, "allow me to introduce myself. I am Claude Cadence, master perfumer *de* Languedoc, and this is Mademoiselle Astell *de Londres*." He lifted the woman's bony hand to his lips. "*Enchanté.*"

The woman's face crinkled into a delighted smile.

After that, their task was simple. She invited them inside and offered them tea and biscuits. Esme watched her slow movements, and leaped up to take the teakettle from her hands. As she finished preparing the repast an odd sensation of rightness settled in her—no doubt caused by the scent of the tea, which happened to be her sister Colleen's favorite.

Married to a Scot for fifty years, Mrs. Wallis had been

widowed for nearly a decade and, as the city overtook her tiny village, had been alone amidst the bustle of modern life. Her only callers, she said, were her husband's younger sister and her nephew, Eustace, although not frequently, as well as a young itinerant laborer who had recently been making repairs to the house.

"Poor Eustace was in such distress when he last visited," she said. "Stomping about the house and grumbling. My nephew has an unsteady temperament."

"Tut-tut," Monsieur Cadence said with a sympathetic shake of his head. "The young are too full of the passions, are they not, madam? They do not understand the beauty of a long, peaceful nap in the sunshine, do they?" With a slight turn of his head, he winked privately at Esme.

"My poor Douglass was so upset, he ran into the closet and hid," Mrs. Wallis said, cuddling the dog in her lap. "I have never seen him do such a thing before."

"What a brute, to frighten the poor little thing," Monsieur Cadence said.

Esme's heart was racing. The dog, Douglass, had taken fondly to Charlie, who had stolen it right out of this house. But it disliked her *nephew?*

"Mrs. Wallis," she said. "What is your nephew's name, if I may?"

"Eustace Smythe-Eggers."

Esme shared a look with the master perfumer.

"Madam," he said to Mrs. Wallis, "I fear that we have a terrible story to tell."

When they had finished, the elderly woman's eyes were

filled with dismay. But swiftly her surprise turned to understanding.

"I should have anticipated it," she said sadly. "Eustace has been pressing me to give him my husband's collection for years. It is worth a fortune, of course. But I haven't been able to bear parting with it. I expect he hoped that without my darling Douglass I would be so despondent that I would simply fade away of loneliness."

"Or perhaps," the Frenchman said, "he intended to hold the poor creature for the ransom?"

"Oh, dear," Mrs. Wallis said. "What a dreadful boy my nephew has turned out to be." She stroked her fingertips along the tiny dog's curly back and it wiggled in happiness.

"What is your husband's collection, Mrs. Wallis?"

"You must come see it."

With tottering steps she started toward the rear of the house. Monsieur Cadence took her arm and they entered a sizable library. From floor to ceiling and all around, the shelves were stacked with books.

"My husband was a scholar. An amateur only. But he spent nearly every shilling of his inheritance on these books. He built this room for his treasures, for many of them you see were quite valuable." She chuckled. "He always said it was grander than Sir Walter Scott's library at Abbotsford. See here, a set of engravers' plates my husband received as a gift for writing a biography of Lord Nelson for His Majesty himself! The images are so delicate, one can almost see the ships' sails billowing in the wind."

"Mrs. Wallis," Esme said, "have you ever considered selling any of these?"

"Years ago I asked my nephew to find a suitable buyer," she said with a weak wave of her hand. "He tried to rush me into selling them to an unworthy man. I was persuaded the man was a professional thief. I told Eustace I would rather the whole collection burn to the ground than to hand it over to a common huckster."

"What if a man who knows books very well, who appreciates them, indeed adores books, were to help you catalogue and curate this collection?" She ran her fingers over the plates that reminded her of the many plates Charlie had commissioned from artists for the books and pamphlets Brittle and Sons produced. "Would you consider employing him for the task?"

"Know you such a scholar willing to take on such a laborious task?"

Esme smiled. "It so happens that I do."

Monsieur Cadence was expected at the final members' session before the party that evening that was to be the finale to the meeting. Instructing the coachman to drive her and the boys wherever they wished, he offered a jaunty tip of his hat, and bid them adieu until anon.

Esme went to the Hart and Rose.

Charlie was not there. Pushing away the ache in her heart telling her that their night together had obviously meant little to him, she gave instructions to the boys.

"Find him, Rory. Then bid him meet me on the bridge to New Town at ten o'clock tonight." The bridge was less than a block from the party venue.

Returning to the hotel, she dressed in her finest frock and walked to the party, her stomach a ball of anxiety.

Standing at the head of the room, Monsieur Poe cleared his throat and everyone fell silent.

"It is my pleasure now," he said to the three dozen men and Esme, "to announce my latest discovery: Mademoiselle Astell."

All eyes fixed on her.

"Who would have imagined such a nose could come from the peasantry, *n'est-ce pas?*" her idol said with a little smirk. "I will be extending to her an invitation to join my school of apprentices in Paris *immédiatement.*"

Applause filled the room and she could feel the heat in her cheeks and she told herself to smile. But abruptly she understood: going to Paris had never been about apprenticing herself to the master perfumer. It had been about living her life fully.

For three years she had endured poor wages and no respect from her employer while nursing a miserable infatuation for a man who never gave her more than a cursory glance. Then for two more years, as she had established Skinner's Perfumery as one of the premier fragrance boutiques in London, barely getting a word of thanks for it, she had mooned over the loss of Charlie. In traveling to Scotland for this meeting, she had been seeking more: laughter, learning, *passion.*

She fully intended to have it all.

"Mademoiselle?" Monsieur Poe said, frowning.

Everybody in the room was waiting for her to speak.

"Thank you, monsieur," she said with confident calm. "I am honored, and delighted to accept your invitation."

Many sincere congratulations later, she was walking through the crisp, clear night toward the bridge. Streetlights lit all in a magical glow. The glow inside her was even brighter.

She did not expect him to come. As the bells of a church far beyond Arthur's Seat tolled ten times, she wrapped her cloak tightly about her and leaned against the railing and breathed in the scents of early spring, and wondered if he were already gone, if a ship had departed from Leith today bound for Boston.

When at the end of the bridge a man appeared in silhouette before a street lamp, she knew it was he by the shape of his shoulders and his solid stance. How different he was now, yet how much the same man. Her stomach was all tumbling pleasure and pain.

"You have not departed yet," she said as he halted a yard away.

"Tomorrow."

"Oh." Of course he was still leaving. "I see that Rory found you."

"I had not planned to come here tonight, Esme."

"Then why did you?"

"I convinced myself that I had enough discipline to prevent myself from touching you if we met."

"And do you?"

"No. You'd better make this quick."

She proffered a letter from Mrs. Wallis. He stepped forward and took it without touching her.

He read, and the pensive tension of his features transformed into pure masculine beauty.

"She is looking forward to seeing you tomorrow morning," Esme said. "You have become something of a hero to her, you know. I think it is mostly because little Douglass adores you. But she is thoroughly impressed with your bravery and good conscience."

"How have you done this?" he said.

"Oh, I put together the clues. But I did not do it alone. Rory and the boys assisted, and Monsieur Cadence. Are you happy with it?"

"Happy? I am *ecstatic*." Grabbing her up in his arms, he spun her around in a circle. She laughed as he set her down.

His mouth on hers abruptly silenced her laughter.

It was a perfect kiss, full of joy and passion and wild desire. His hands tangled in her hair and hers spread over his waistcoat, and the moonlight and starlight and light in her heart made her feel thoroughly enchanted.

She pulled away first.

"Esme, thank you. I don't think—" His chest rose hard but he did not continue.

"What?"

"No one has ever done anything like this for me before."

"Then it was high time," she said, tasting the flavor of him on her lips and taking a step away from his strong arms and taut jaw and beautiful eyes that were showing her the very *last* thing she wanted to see now.

"Will you stay?" he said.

Beneath her ribs, happiness and misery together tinkled like hollow little crystal glasses shattering.

"Stay?" She forced the word over her tongue.

"Here in Edinburgh. While I do this project."

"Tomorrow I am leaving for London."

He moved close again.

"Delay your journey. Please."

She shook her head and her eyes were prickling. She swallowed back the threatening tears.

"I cannot," she said.

"You have done this, Esme. You have made this happen. I want to share it with you."

"I have been offered an apprenticeship, the post I sought in coming here. My dream is waiting for me in Paris."

His smile was so genuine.

"Congratulations, madam master perfumer," he said, smiling, but his voice was not entirely even.

"It is everything I have ever wanted." *Except him.* "Hopefully within a year I will be able to support my sisters and mother. I am so happy, Charlie."

"Then I must be happy as well." He lifted both of her hands to his lips, and kissed one, then the other. "This is finally goodbye."

Her throat had closed entirely; she nodded.

"Esme, you are an extraordinary person. Strong, courageous, intelligent." His eyes were shining peculiarly. "Adventuresome."

She tried to smile. "I suppose I would be an excellent pirate, then."

"No. You are far too generous. You have the heart of a hero."

That heart was beating painfully fast and hard now. She hardly knew what to say.

Bending his head, he kissed her. It was tender, a kiss of friendship and admiration, and of parting. She closed her eyes and imprinted on her memory his flavor, texture, and heat to hold and keep for the solitary days to come.

"May your dreams continue to come true, Esme Astell," he said close to her cheek.

Then he was gone, across the bridge and into the darkness. And she was alone again with her aching heart and singing head and the scent of nighttime all around.

CHAPTER ELEVEN

The following morning, Charlie called on Mrs. Wallis. She met him with astonishing forgiveness, as well as the announcement that she had informed the police that wee Douglass had never in fact been stolen. Then they made plans for her husband's library. Charlie departed his new patron's house moderately bemused, yet feeling more like a man of worthwhile purpose than he had in years.

His next call was to the home of Mr. Eustace Smythe-Eggers.

A tulip with bombastic habits of speech, he recognized Charlie from the party but still denied ever having had possession of the dog. Five minutes later, during which Charlie painted a detailed portrait of Smythe-Eggers's future were he to ever threaten Mrs. Wallis again, the man was on his knees expostulating at volume.

"Never meant to harm the little thing! Only meant to bend Auntie's attention toward *me*. Then I'd happen to find the wee critter all of the sudden, and be the hero of the day.

Auntie can't leave her riches to a *dog*. Thought I'd remind her of that."

After several more minutes of the man's groveling, Charlie wrested from him a pathetic promise to never again harm his aunt or her pet. Adding that he would know if Smythe-Eggers consorted with thieves again, he took his leave.

Several days later, he found a buyer for the engravers' plates: a bookmaker with whom he had once worked on an author's project, who promised to use the magnificent works to illustrate the latest collection of Lord Nelson's personal letters, and who paid him a sum far beyond the plates' worth.

When Charlie told Mrs. Wallis the news, she insisted he add the difference in the asking and selling prices to his commission.

"I cannot."

"Yet you must, dearie," she said, patting his hand as though he were a schoolboy.

He used the money to purchase supplies to repair the widow's house.

News of the valuable collection spread rapidly. Two days later he parted with a rare quarto at twice its worth. Mr. Wallis had been particularly fond of naval history, and the current fashion for tales of the heroics of naval men made the collection especially desirable to scholars, collectors, and dilettantes alike. Charlie's intimate knowledge of sailing made advertising the treasures particularly easy.

When within a fortnight Mrs. Wallis received a letter from a hundred miles away asking after a particular text, Charlie knew the collection was destined to net her thousands. He was satisfied. Fulfilled. Doing what he loved most and helping a woman who needed his help while instructing Rory and the boys in repairs of her house and grounds, and paying them well for it.

Pate had sailed, satisfied with the three hundred shiny guineas Charlie had paid for his freedom. That threat was behind him too.

After nearly two years, his life had begun again, this time under no other man's thumb—not his father's or brother's or captain's. Finally he was his own man.

Yet every night for fourteen nights after he had met Esme on that bridge, he found himself at the Hart and Rose, sitting at the corner table with a cup of tea before him.

He hated tea.

Rather, he *had*. Now he could not smell it without recalling her story about her sisters and her insistence that scent was the quickest access to memories, and wanting her—her quick smile, her twinkling eyes that revealed an irrepressibly optimistic nature, her tenacity and strength in adversity, the flavor of her mouth, and the caress of her hands on his skin. Every time he smelled tea now, forever, he would want her.

He would want her all the other moments of every day, too.

A fortnight earlier Rory had assured him that he had watched her leave the hotel on foot and carrying her luggage, and walk to the posting house and board the mail coach for London.

Shortly she would be on her way to Paris. She had helped him, made love to him, but as ever, she was self-possessed, confident, independent. She did not need a man marked with the symbols of his captivity, a man with no certain future.

Rising from the table and leaving coins beside the untouched tea, he started toward the pub's door. The boarding-house proprietress stood in the aperture looking directly at him.

"There you be, scapegrace!" She bustled toward him.

"I beg your pardon, madam?"

"Dinna be puttin' on airs with me! Edna McDade knows a gay deceiver when she sees him leap out o' a lass's window."

"You saw that, did you?"

"I know what goes on under my own roof, lad," she said with puffy indignation.

"I beg your pardon, ma'am." He bowed, not needing a tongue-lashing at present but knowing he fully deserved it. "I assure you, it was all in innocence." *Partly.*

"Innocence, ha! But in my day I'd a highboy or two, myself. I'll no' be ringin' a peal o'er your head."

"That is a relief, I admit."

"But I'll no' be givin' board to them who canna pay for it, neither," she declared.

"That seems fiscally wise," he said. "I am not clear, however, as to how that policy relates to me."

"Aye?" she said, her eyes narrowing to slits. "Next you'll be claimin' you've ne'er seen the rips come beggin' at my door!"

"Rips?"

"Aha, there be a young jackanapes!" She wagged her finger then gestured into the street. "Ogle them for yourself, then vow you've no' put them up to their wily ways."

Curious, he followed her from the pub. As dusk fell over the cobbles, walkers and riders hurried along the street, seeking warmth from the chill spring evening. Huddled together and entirely immobile among the bustle were two young women carrying bandboxes and looking positively beleaguered.

"They'll no' search the likes o' my house!" Mrs. McDade declared.

"Search your house?" he said.

"Insistin' on it! I told them I'd allow a pair o' fleas to come inside afore I'd give them a room gratis."

The young women's homespun gowns, worn cloaks, and straw bonnets marked them from the countryside. Most likely they hoped to barter for a room as they bartered at country markets.

Charlie suppressed a smile, but an alien sensation was gathering in his chest.

Laughter.

Perhaps only a chuckle. But laughter nonetheless.

"Mrs. McDade," he said, marveling at the unfamiliar feeling, "I suspect this is merely a misunderstanding." Speaking the words—words so much like the negotiating he'd had to do time and again with customers whom his brother had sweet-talked into befuddlement or anger—he felt like himself again. Yet newer. Stronger.

Perhaps once Mrs. Wallis's library was curated and catalogued for scholars' use, he would go to America after all. A land of promise, they called it. If it could promise he would not feel pain beneath his ribs every time he thought of Esme, he would board the first westward-sailing ship.

"Will you allow me to assist in this negotiation?" he said.

"I'll have none o' your niceties, sir! Only take these raga-muffins out o' my sight."

"We are not ragamuffins, and we have not asked to have a room without paying for it," the taller girl said in an unmis-takably English voice, although with a northern cadence that struck a chord of familiarity in him.

She turned to him and Charlie's heart did a full stop.

"As I've already said, we have traveled here to find our sister," she said, "who wrote to us that she was staying at this boardinghouse. We merely wish to see her."

"You'll no' be comin' into my house with those muddy shoes," Mrs. McDade exclaimed.

"We have only just come from the coach. We haven't yet had time to wash up."

"Wash up! I'll be washin' my hands o' *you*. Here be the jackanapes," she declared with a gesture at him. "Ask *him* o' your sister's whereabouts." She marched back into the boardinghouse and shut the door.

"Ladies," he said with a quaver he could not control. "May I invite you to take some refreshment in the public house here?"

"Oh! You are English!" she said in a voice that was too familiar, from lips the same shape as the lips of the woman he loved. "What a relief it is to speak with an Englishman again. We have barely understood anybody in *days*."

"Perhaps, after you have rested, you will allow me to assist you in finding a more accommodating situation in the neighborhood?"

"Thank you, sir! We will be very grateful. My sister and I have had *such* a time of it," she said as she took the girl's arm. "There was a terrible storm that slowed the mail coach from Leeds so that we missed our connection and were obliged to wait two days for the next." The words poured out of her, distress woven into every syllable. "But we had no funds for the inn and so we slept in a barn. The farmer was very kindly, and traded the haystack for milking the following morning."

"I see," he murmured, seating them at a table beside the blazing hearth and silently thanking God for Edna Mc-Dade's attention to comings and goings. The girls' eyes were full of relief as he gestured the barkeep to serve them.

"Then there were no more places inside," the elder sister continued without encouragement, "so my sister and I were obliged to ride atop, and Colleen is not always well in bright sunlight, but then it rained again—a blessing even though we got wet through. Thus our current state. I don't blame Mrs. McDade for refusing us entry. In truth, we came without making any preparations for the journey, especially since neither of us has ever traveled anywhere before and hadn't any idea what to expect. But we were *desperate* to find our sister."

"Were you?"

"Oh, yes." She nodded vigorously. "We used our every penny to come here. She writes to us so frequently that when we received the letter she wrote after her second day in Edinburgh we knew something was horribly wrong."

"Wrong?" His heart was beating at a swift pace.

"She sounded so thoroughly distressed, saying that the man she had loved for years was *not* dead after all and that she was so confused but all she could think was that she must help him because if something awful happened to him—if he were in trouble of some sort, which it seemed he was—she would never live happily again. But she was so determined to succeed at the project that brought her to Edinburgh, and Mama wept and said we must come here now, so that she was not all alone facing these challenges. Our sister dislikes being alone, you see, terribly, and we miss her dreadfully too. But she is so strong, and—Oh, goodness, you must think me a springtime brook to babble on and on! How kind you are. I'm certain after we drink this tea we will be able to see to ourselves. I cannot understand why Mrs. McDade fetched you to assist us but we are truly grateful for—Sir? Are you all right?"

For years.

She had loved him for *years*?

"Yes," he managed.

No.

She had loved him for years. How could he have not realized it? How could he have been so preoccupied with proving himself a better man than his brother, and so thoroughly blind to everything else, that he could have seen her every week for years and not *known*?

"Dear me," her sister said. "I have talked too much. I beg your pardon, sir."

"Miss Mary Astell, I believe?" he said unsteadily, then turning to her sister: "Miss Colleen?"

Their eyes, which were the same lovely shade of blue-gray as Esme's, popped wide.

"Yes," Mary said.

Colleen nodded.

"Your sister set off for London fourteen days ago. Allow me, if you will, to find lodgings for you today. Then after you are suitably rested, I will hire a private carriage to take you home, or to London, as you wish."

"You *know* our sister?"

Knew her. Loved her. One and the same.

"Yes," he said. "I am Charles Brittle."

And for the first time in twenty-two months, he believed it.

CHAPTER TWELVE

June 1823
Gracechurch Street
London, England

Esme placed the final items in her traveling trunk, closed the latch, then stood back and surveyed her empty side of the room. Only one object remained on her bed: the letter from her sisters that she had read so many times it had gotten worn out from reading.

When she had received it, she had not been surprised. Of course Charlie had found them wonderful lodgings, and of course he had paid for their journey home, and of course he had been the perfect gentleman, seeing to their comforts and making them happy.

How exactly he had come to encounter and then recognize them was not entirely clear: Mary's letter referred vaguely to nasty Mrs. McDade and a scene on the street. But it hardly mattered. He had helped them because that was simply what he did. He was wonderful.

Picking up the letter for the last time, she pressed it to her lips, then cast it upon the grate. The simmering coals swallowed it in a quick burst of flame.

She sniffed.

"Are you so despondent to leave that you are weeping?" Adela said behind her.

Esme's flatmate stood in the doorway to their bedchamber.

"Not at all." Only to leave him behind, once and for all. Where she was going now, she would begin anew. No more useless infatuations. No more unrequited love. No more heartbreak. Only learning and creating and grand adventure.

Adela threw her arms around her and hugged her tightly.

"Well, I will miss you," Adela declared. "And so will Minnie. And I'll wager nasty Josiah Junior will miss you too, even if he does not realize it. That lecher has been eyeing you since the moment you returned from Scot—Oh!" She released Esme and darted around her to the window. "Good Lord," she exclaimed. "It's Charlie Brittle!"

Esme's heart did a thick, hard turnabout. She went to the window and over Adela's shoulder looked down into the street.

There he was, standing before the door of his family's print shop, beneath the sign that read Brittle and Sons, Printers and looking up at her window as she had always dreamed, wished, and hoped he would yet never had.

"He's seen me!" Adela grabbed the broken latch and flung open the window. "Charlie!" she shouted into the street.

"Good day, Adela," he said.

"Where have you *been?*" Adela called down. People walking and riding by glanced at her, then at him.

"I will be glad to tell you. But first, would you be so kind as to ask Miss Astell if she will allow me a moment of her time?"

Adela swung her head around and pinned Esme with a wide-eyed stare. Esme swallowed over her careening heartbeats, nodded at him, and went out of the room and down the stairs. Opening the door onto the street she came face-to-face with him.

The dye had gone from his hair and it was rakishly long now and a bit tousled, the sandy blond striated with gold. His beautiful eyes looked fierce.

"Why aren't you in Paris?"

"Good day to you too, sir."

"*Why aren't you in Paris?*"

"I am not going to Paris."

"But it is your dream."

"It was. But I realized it was the wrong dream. I am going to Provence, where I will study with Monsieur Cadence, who has taken me on as his apprentice."

"Are you happy with this?"

"Yes. Very, very happy."

His shoulders seemed to settle. "Then I am happy as well."

"Why are you here? Shouldn't you be in Edinburgh? Or already on your way to America?"

"No. Esme, I am sorry I am so late."

"Late? Late for what?"

"I would have been here sooner, but I spent the past several weeks searching for Pate."

"Pate! But *why?*"

"I had to free the others he held captive."

It felt as though someone were squeezing her heart. Of course he had risked his freedom for that. "Did you succeed?"

"Yes, although not as I expected. Esme, he was dying. He had known he was dying for months, long before we made port in Scotland. When I found him, he barely had enough breath to tell me he was leaving everything to me—his ship, his gold, his property. Everything."

She gaped.

"That was my reaction too," he said. "He said the dog, the money, it had all been a test."

"A test of what?"

"Of my mettle. My resourcefulness. My desperation to be free of him, perhaps. I don't know. He died without explaining."

"I—I don't know what to say. I will not wish you my sympathy. But, Charlie, what will you do with this ill-gotten wealth?"

"I have given it to charitable foundations, all but a parcel of land on the coast of Devonshire that his solicitor insists was kept scrupulously free of any taint of criminal gains. Apparently," he said with a slight smile, "it was his grandmother's property and Pate had a fondness for her good opinion of him."

She laughed. "How remarkable."

"But when I said I was sorry for being late," he said, "I

meant five years late. I am sorry, Esme, that in all those years when you were only four doors away, I never told you—showed you—how I felt about you."

"About . . . *me?*" she whispered.

"I never looked at you," he said. "I never *let* myself look at you, not after the first few months after you arrived in London when each time I looked at you I got confused."

"What do you mean, confused?"

"If you knew how many times my heart said, 'carry those heavy packages for her' or 'throw your coat over that puddle before she wets her feet' or 'offer to repair the broken window in her flat' while my hands said, 'grab her and pin her against the wall and kiss her'—but my head said 'she couldn't want you.' So quiet and self-possessed, you didn't need helping or protecting—or *me.* You didn't need anyone."

"Everyone needs someone," she said.

"I know one thing: that I need you. I am in love with you, Esme. Perhaps you will think me too hasty in expressing my—"

Grabbing his lapel, she pressed her body to his and with her other hand pulled him down to kiss her. Then his arms were wrapped around her and her arms were twined about his neck and their mouths were deliriously declaring their love in hungry kisses and tender kisses and yet more rapturous kisses.

"Will you go to live in Devonshire now?" she eventually said with the little breath she had remaining.

He looked into her eyes. "I will go wherever you go. If you will have me."

With a burst of joyful laughter and further enthusiastic kisses she showed him how thoroughly she would have him at the first possible opportunity.

"But what of Mrs. Wallis and her collection?" she said. "Will you abandon her?"

"She and her collection are in good hands. After agreeing to sell the most valuable pieces, she has decided to keep the remainder and hire a quartet of lads to index it for the use of scholars."

"A quartet. Rory and the boys! But do they even read?"

He smiled.

"Oh, that is her *actual* project," she said. "She intends to school them."

"Under cover of honest work."

She ran a fingertip along his jaw.

"And you, pirate, what honest work will you do now that you are a free man?"

"I believe I will look for work in France. Southern France, in particular. I suspect someone there has need of a man who can set type, curate books, and swab decks."

She lifted her face to be kissed and then whispered into his ear the words she had whispered against the window pane in her bedchamber and the pillow and the sweet summer wind hundreds of times: "I love you, Charles Westley Brittle."

EPILOGUE

November 1823
Arles, Southern France

With her sisters tending Monsieur Cadence's shop, it was Esme's delight to spend her days mixing potions in the workshop alongside her teacher and soaking up the encyclopedic knowledge he imparted to her. When he traveled, which he did often, he instructed Esme to work if necessary, but mostly to spend time enjoying the wonders of town and countryside, wandering byways and pastures and hills and dells to discover scents and collect samples that might be used in the workshop.

A master perfumer, he insisted, never ceased searching for not only the perfect combination of scents, but also the perfect sources.

Occasionally on such languid mornings, she chose to explore the sources of scent—and touch, and sound, and flavor—in her own bed.

"You, my wife," Charlie murmured as he bent his head

to place kisses one after another on her neck and shoulder, "grow more exceedingly beautiful each day."

Threading her fingers through his roguishly long hair, she welcomed the direction that his mouth was taking: southward.

"Perhaps that is because I am exceedingly happy," she said.

He looked up from his ministrations of her exceedingly happy flesh. His lips were damp, as was her nipple now, and his eyes were full of love and—stunningly—lust too.

"Beautiful," he repeated.

"And hungry," she added. Then she wiggled her brows to indicate exactly how hungry, so that he would not mistake it and dash off to fetch her chocolate and bread.

Shortly, he was satisfying her hunger wonderfully well.

Afterward, stretching her body languorously against his, and loving that his strong hands were still holding her, she decided it was finally time for chocolate and bread.

"Today is a holiday," she said with a smile.

"Every day that I awake with you is a holiday," he said, nuzzling behind her ear, where she especially liked him to nuzzle.

"Where shall we go?"

"You: to wherever you wish, be it field or lake or village or garden," he said muffled against her skin, cupping his palm rather casually around her buttock. "I: you already know to where."

"Your work will never be finished," she said, trailing her fingertips down his arm.

"We shall see."

Upon their arrival in Provence months earlier, as Esme began her studies with the master perfumer, Charlie had offered to see to Monsieur Cadence's account ledgers, which he had done with his usual competence. But they had not been there a fortnight when a grandly garbed man strode into the workshop and lamented to the perfumer that his lady required a fragrance to overcome the scent of centuries of dust.

"Monsieur Cadence, my collection shall be the finest in France," he had declared in round Gallic tones, then frowned. "But my responsibilities, alas, are too many to be able to tend to it suitably, and it languishes, dear monsieur. It languishes!" He shook his head. "I must depart, for this very week the king expects me at court until the spring. If only I could find a man who would cherish my treasure as I do! A man of intelligence and sense, whom I could trust."

The lamenter, it turned out, was a count whose house typically remained empty throughout the year, as he and his countess were more often at court or abroad than at home. Even then they had more than one house in France, and this one only a mile distant from town was used principally to store the count's treasured collection.

Monsieur Cadence replied that he knew of such a trustworthy man, and the man could ride to the house that very day if the count desired. The count did desire it, and Charlie went to meet him.

The house was, in fact, a castle set at the apex of two hundred acres of breathtaking domain, and the count's treasure was one for which Charles Westley Brittle was the ideal care-taker.

"The countess's note to me yesterday complained of her husband purchasing yet another estate's collection," Esme said now.

Charlie lifted his head and smiled slowly, beautifully. "Did he? I've heard nothing of it yet."

"No doubt it will arrive just as the last did, in haphazard bundles and dusty crates. You will be weeks sorting them all."

He was kissing her jaw and throat again and she touched the tips of her fingers to his back, playing upon the scars as upon harp strings.

"I should like you to take me there," she said.

"You have been there dozens of times," he said, smoothing his palm along her side and leaning back onto his shoulder. "And it is only downstairs. You already know the way."

"I don't mean *lead* me," she said. "I mean take me."

This time he understood her meaning with gratifying speed. The corner of his mouth hitched up.

"Would you?" he said.

She could not withhold her grin.

His hand came around the back of her head and he kissed her firmly, which she understood as assent.

Then he climbed from the bed and crossed their cozy little bedchamber in the chateau's topmost turret. Curling up around a pillow, she watched as he cupped his hands together in the washbowl and splashed water over his face, then ran his fingers through his hair and took a linen to his chest where the water trickled down in rivulets. As he moved, the muscles shifted and the ropes about his arms appeared to twist.

He rarely acknowledged aloud the paint or the scars. But when she kissed him where ink or puckers marked his skin, sometimes he looked at her with such awe, such unfiltered adoration, that she was obliged to swallow tears.

He pulled on a shirt, tightening the cuffs with buttons, and then donned trousers and the remainder of his garments. He glanced at her.

"Will you loll about here all day, my lady of leisure?"

He liked to tease her for her preference to remain abed so long after waking. He had no idea that each morning this was her special gift to herself, to watch him bathe and dress.

"Not at all," she said. "I have the countess's fragrance to complete, and the last of the lavender to harvest as well."

"Come find me after you are finished," he said, tying his cravat as neatly as though he were looking in a mirror though he was looking at her. The slightest crease appeared in his cheek. "If you wish."

When he left the chamber she flopped onto her back and smiled at the canopy above her and then out the window at the day rising in soft mists over the countryside.

An hour later, dressed and breakfasted, she drove the gig into town and greeted her sisters in the shop.

Monsieur Cadence's widowed sister lived above the perfume shop, and when Mary and Colleen had arrived two months earlier she had welcomed them with open arms. They had both taken to shopkeeping with enthusiastic glee.

Each day they looked rounder and more content than the day before.

"See, Esme, to what our sister has turned her talents," Mary said, her feather duster whisking along a shelf of crystal bottles.

Colleen was leaning over a slab of wood, a tool in hand. Half of Monsieur Cadence's name was already carved into the wood in scrolling letters.

"How wonderful!" Esme exclaimed. "I had no idea you could do such a thing, Collie."

"N-neither had I," Colleen said, head jiggling as she smiled but her hand steady on the tool. She propped the new shop marquee up on her knees. "I shall p-p-paint it too. G-gold and blue and g-green. D-d-do you l-like it?"

"Yes! And I know Monsieur Cadence will too."

"Sp-splendid!"

Esme wrapped her arms about her youngest sister and they embraced and laughed. Laughter and embraces were regular features to every day now.

"There is another letter from Mama," Mary said. "She is well. Pious as ever." She rolled her eyes, then grinned.

The day Mary and Colleen had set off for France, their mother had set off for Ireland. There she had entered a convent and, knowing that all three of her daughters were safe from her brother-in-law and happy, was finally content.

Esme went into the workshop and set about her many tasks happily.

But when midday turned to afternoon and the sky sparkled with early winter's brilliance and the air smelled more of the cool breeze off the hills than smoke from morning fires, she slipped out the rear door, hitched the horse to the gig, and drove home.

She found her husband exactly where she expected: in the library.

A two-story chamber of grand proportions, with a balustrade that ran the length of a second story accessed by spiral stairs, it was lined with bookshelves, three-quarters of which were filled with volumes bound in colorful gilded leather. As anticipated, a mountain of crates decorated one corner. Two that were open revealed books packed in straw, each volume wrapped carefully in oil cloth. Sunlight filtered in through partially drawn draperies hung at Charlie's request to protect the count's precious collection of hundreds of antique books and manuscripts, which Charlie was repairing, preserving, and indexing.

From the mezzanine, without lifting his attention from the book in his hands, he said, "More than I imagined."

She walked to the base of the stairs. "What is more than you imagined?"

He closed the book, set it on a shelf, and came to the top of the stairs.

"The hours that would pass before you arrived," he said.

Grasping the railing with both of her hands, she leaned forward and looked up at him.

"But you knew I would eventually arrive."

He lifted a single brow. "I hoped."

A moment later she was up the stairs and in his arms.

Turning her back against the shelf, he trapped her there

with his body and said above her eagerly lifted lips, "Why here?"

She wrapped her arms around his shoulders. "Do you object?"

"Never. Anywhere." As though to prove it he brought his hips against hers and made her thoroughly aware of his eagerness as well. "I simply wondered why."

"Because this project makes you happy," she said, welcoming his mouth on her neck and his hands gathering up her skirts. "And I love that you are happy."

"I needn't have this project to be happy, Esme," he said, his hands on her thighs beneath her gown. "You are all that I need."

"All right. How about this as a reason: because this is the only place in the chateau in which we have not yet made love."

"You don't say?"

"To be remedied momentarily, I trust."

"Don't rush me, madam," he said, touching her so that she was clinging to him and making sounds of pleasure against his mouth. "There is a woman here to be thoroughly pleased."

"*Taken.*" She dissolved in laughter.

"Loved," he said quite seriously.

"Oh, Charlie—"

He kissed her and then showed her that, without question, he could satisfy all of those at once.

A Note from Katharine

I hope you enjoyed Esme and Charlie's romance! I had so much fun writing it.

If you are new to my books, welcome! You can find more of Charlie and Esme in the prequel to *The Pirate & I*, my novella, *The Scoundrel & I*, featuring Gabrielle and her heroic naval captain.

Princess Bride fans will undoubtedly have recognized my allusions in this novella to that wonderful film. As to the song that Charlie sings to Esme, "Red is the Rose": it is an old Irish folk song. I particularly recommend the lovely recording of it by The High Kings.

The great—rather, *terrible*—age of piracy that we often hear about encompassed the seventeenth and eighteenth centuries. But in the early nineteenth century pirates still abounded, and those who did were especially wily since the English navy had grown extraordinarily powerful.

Speaking of the king's navy: victorious naval commander

and Scotland's notorious and darkly reclusive lord, Gabriel Hume, the Devil's Duke, returns in *The Duke*, coming September 2017 from Avon Books. In *The Duke* you'll also see Rory Markum and Edinburgh again, as well as the breathtaking Scottish countryside studded with magnificent castles. (A Scottish castle, it turns out, is the ideal place for a notorious duke to steal a dalliance with a persistent English-woman he had thought to never see again.)

Many thanks to my readers, who make writing love stories so much fun, and especially to The Princesses, the best street team in the world. To the wonderful people who helped me prepare Esme and Charlie's romance for publication, I send up cheers of joy and thanks: Marcia Abercrombie, Sandie Blaise, Anne Brophy, Georgann T. Brophy, Georgie C. Brophy, Noah Brophy, Maria Fairchild, Donna Finlay, Meg Huliston, Jenn LeBlanc, Mary B. Marcus, and Teresa Moore. I extend very special thanks as well to Elizabeth B. Dunn and her colleagues at Duke University's David M. Rubenstein Rare Book & Manuscript Library.

Always for my editor, Lucia Macro, and everybody at Avon—including Carolyn Coons, Angela Craft, Shawn Nicholls, Caroline Perny, and the infinitely patient and gracious production and art departments—and for my agent Kimberly Whalen, I am deeply grateful.

Finally, profound thanks to my husband, my son, and my Idaho, whose love and assistance make me a better writer and a very happy human.

For more about my books and series, I hope you will visit me at my website, www.KatharineAshe.com. I love hearing from readers.

And now, a glimpse of that notorious duke and persistent Englishwoman at the very same ball that Esme and Charlie visited . . .

THE DUKE

The Assembly Rooms
Port of Leith, Scotland

"You do not frighten me." She snipped the syllables to hide their quaver.

His gaze that was black in the dim light scanned her face—her cheeks and hair and lips and chin.

"Then you are unique among women," he rumbled. "Now, remove that key from your bodice and open the door."

"Why won't you speak with me?" This was frankly terrifying. She had not anticipated this or planned for any scenario like this. She had imagined that when she finally cornered him he would act like a regular person and converse—unwisely, she realized belatedly. He had never been anything like a regular person, after all.

"Five and a half years, yet not even a little small talk?" she said. "Come now. Let us give it a try. I will start. I hear you have become a duke. And an abductor of innocent maidens. And possibly a practitioner of the dark arts. How do you find all of that?"

"Lass." The word was a warning shift of tectonic plates. "Open the door now or I'll be taking that key."

"You cannot deter me, Urisk." Now her voice quivered quite obviously. "Either you will sit down here now and answer my questions until I have asked them all, or you will in fact be obliged to take the key from me."

In the darkness, the gleam in his eyes was like a blade.

"If you insist," he said as though he whispered in her ear.

Her heart slammed into her lungs.

His hand surrounded her hip.

She gasped.

Large and strong, his five fingers and broad palm took complete possession of her flesh. He was not smiling.

"The key now," he said very deeply. His fingers moved on her buttock. Not painfully. Rather, stroking, kneading as though she were bread dough.

She swallowed over the shock clogging her throat.

"No," she croaked.

He bent his head and in the murky silence in which the gay music of the ball was only a distant echo, she could hear his breathing, each inhale and exhale a perfectly controlled statement of composure.

"You are certain?" he said as calmly as though he were asking if she preferred tea to coffee.

"Yes."

His hand slid up her side and wrapped around her waist.

"What are you *doing?*" she rasped.

His thumb stroked along the ridge of her lowest rib and a horrible—*wonderful*—cascade of pleasure descended inside her.

"Getting closer to that key."

About the Author

KATHARINE ASHE is the award-winning author of historical romances that reviewers call "intensely lush" and "sensationally intelligent," including *How to Be a Proper Lady*, an Amazon Editors' Choice for the 10 Best Books of the Year in Romance, and *My Lady, My Lord* and *How to Marry a Highlander*, 2015 and 2014 finalists for the prestigious RITA® Award of the Romance Writers of America. Her books are recommended by *Publishers Weekly*, *Woman's World* magazine, *Booklist*, *Library Journal*, *Kirkus Reviews*, Barnes & Noble, All About Romance, and many others, and translated into languages across the world.

Katharine lives in the wonderfully warm southeast with her beloved husband, son, dog, and a garden she likes to call romantic rather than unkempt. A professor of European history, she writes fiction because she thinks modern readers deserve grand adventures and breathtaking sensuality too. For more about Katharine's books, please visit www.KatharineAshe.com or write to her at PO Box 51702, Durham, North Carolina 27717.

Dear Reader,

I hope you liked the latest romance from Avon Impulse! If you're looking for another steamy, fun, emotional read, be sure to check out some of our upcoming titles.

If you're a fan of historical romance, get excited! We have two new novellas from beloved Avon authors coming in August. JUST ANOTHER VISCOUNT IN LOVE by Vivienne Lorret is a charming story about an unlucky-in-love Viscount who just wants to find a wife. But every lady he pursues ends up married to another . . . until he meets Miss Gemma Desmond and he vows not to let this woman slip through his fingers! This is a delightful, witty story that will appeal to any/all historical romances fans—even if you've never read Viv before!

We also have a fabulous new story from Lorraine Heath! GENTLEMEN PREFER HEIRESSES is a new story in her Scandalous Gentlemen of St. James series. The second son of a Duke has no reason to give up his wild ways and marry, but when an American heiress catches his eye, the prospect of marriage seems much more appealing. As any true #Heathen (a Lorraine Heath superfan!) knows, her books are deeply emotional and always end with a glorious HEA. This novella is no different!

Never fear contemporary romance fans . . . we didn't forget about you! Tracey Livesay is back at the end of August with LOVE WILL ALWAYS REMEMBER, a fun and sexy new novel with a While You Were Sleeping spin! When a woman awakens from a coma with no memories from the past six years, she's delighted to learn a handsome, celebrity chef is her fiancée . . . or is he? Don't miss this wonderful diverse romance that will have you sighing with happiness!

You can purchase any of these titles by clicking the links above or by visiting our website, www.AvonRomance.com. Thank you for loving romance as much as we do . . . enjoy!

Sincerely,

Nicole Fischer

Editorial Director

Avon Impulse

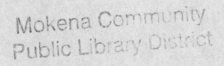